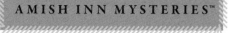

Law &
Old Order

Jan Fields

Annie's®

AnniesFiction.com

Library of Congress-in-Publication Data
Law & Old Order / by Jan Fields
p. cm.
I. Title
                          2016952116

AnniesFiction.com
(800) 282-6643
Amish Inn Mysteries™
Series Creator: Shari Lohner
Series Editors: Lorie Jones and Shari Lohner
Cover Illustrator: Kelley McMorris

10 11 12 13 14 | Printed in China | 9 8 7 6 5 4 3 2 1

1

"You're in danger."

Liz Eckardt stood in the middle of the Olde Mansion Inn's foyer, resisting the urge to simply turn and run from the tiny woman in front of her because a good innkeeper should never flee from her guests. Liz cast a glance toward the heavy front door, hoping desperately for a new guest to arrive early and save her from the strange conversation she found herself trapped in once again. "I am?"

Harriet Vale closed the distance between them, stepping near enough for the tip of her sensible walking shoes to touch Liz's open-toed flats. Among other things, the eccentric, elderly woman was a close talker. At least Harriet's breath always smelled pleasantly of mint.

As she offered her best smile, Liz reminded herself that she loved being an innkeeper in the quaint town of Pleasant Creek, Indiana. She never, ever missed her hectic days as a corporate patent attorney in Boston. Really, she didn't.

"You are. That's what my dream showed me." Harriet peered at Liz with shining dark eyes magnified by cat-eye glasses.

Liz stifled a groan. This would be the third prophetic dream she'd heard since Harriet checked in nine days ago. At first, Liz had been excited that Harriet planned to stay two weeks since guests who booked long visits often had beautiful quilt projects that inspired Liz's own quilting efforts. Harriet was a talented quilter, but her conversations often drifted toward imagined signs of doom and quirky dreams. Liz never knew quite how to respond to Harriet's confusing predictions.

"Dreams can certainly be unusual," Liz said.

"This one was revealed to me as a warning for you," Harriet said, lowering her voice to an intense, if slightly shaky, whisper. "You were being menaced by a gray dog that barked and snapped at you. The dog had sparkling green eyes. You weren't afraid though."

"Good," Liz said brightly. At least she was brave in the odd dream.

"Unfortunately, a giant stone squashed you."

Liz blinked at her bright-eyed guest. "I was squashed? You think that's prophetic? I don't believe I'm in danger of being squashed by a stone here in Pleasant Creek. And the only dog I'm around regularly isn't exactly menacing." She gestured toward the English bulldog who lay on the floor with his nose pointed toward the front door in case any entering guests wanted to slip him a treat. Beans was more decor than pet most of the time.

"Dreams are often symbolic. This one probably is too. I would be careful of conflict with an aggressive person who crushes your spirit." Harriet's look of disapproval dissolved into a sweet expression. She resembled someone who would share fresh-baked cookies with you, not half-baked dream analysis. "I want you to stay safe."

"Thank you," Liz said. "I'll keep your dream in mind. I do try to avoid conflict with aggressive people." *Not that I'm always successful.*

Liz inched to the doorway leading to the library, which gave her an idea. She motioned toward the next room. "I need to step in here and see if the room needs dusting. Books are such dust magnets. Thanks again for the warning." She practically threw herself through the doorway.

"I'll let you know if I get any further insight from my afternoon nap," Harriet called after her. Then Liz heard the light tap of the woman's shoes as she crossed the foyer.

Sighing in relief, Liz leaned against one of the tall, built-in bookshelves. She swept a hand along the edge of the nearest shelf and looked at her fingers. As she'd expected, there wasn't a speck of dust. Liz had the most amazing housekeeper on the planet. Even though Sarah Borkholder worked only part-time, the young Amish woman kept the inn sparkling.

As if summoned by Liz's thoughts, Sarah poked her head into the library. "There is a problem upstairs, Miss Eckardt."

"A problem?"

"The bathroom in the Rose of Sharon Room." Sarah dropped her quiet voice even lower. "The toilet is stopped up."

Liz groaned. "I thought we'd finally gotten ahead of plumbing problems."

"I do not think this is the fault of the plumbing," Sarah replied. "Mrs. Johns said her daughter accidentally dropped something into the toilet."

"Did she say what that something could be?"

The corner of Sarah's mouth twitched, but she kept a completely straight face otherwise. "Apparently, her quilt project."

"I see. I'll take care of it." *And I deserve it.* Normally, Liz's guests checked into the inn for a quilting holiday and didn't ask if children were permitted. But when Courtney Johns called to reserve a room, she'd assured Liz that her eight-year-old daughter, Brya, was excited to learn quilting. The woman had made the quilting retreat sound like a wonderland of bonding time.

So far, the stay had been more nightmare than wonderland with several examples of Brya's mischief, all stemming from her disapproval of her mom's quilting plans.

When Liz reached the second floor, she knocked on the door of the Rose of Sharon Room.

The door opened instantly. The young mother's frizzy blonde hair seemed more out of control than it had been at breakfast, as if she'd been pulling at it. Liz imagined she'd be pulling at her own hair if the wayward Brya were her daughter. Years ago, Liz's godson had been a similar age when he'd moved in with Liz after the death of his parents, but Liz didn't remember nearly so much mischief from Steve, even though he'd had more reasons for acting out.

Courtney smoothed the front of her pale pink sleeveless sweater as she backed away from the door. "I'm sorry for the accident. I cannot imagine how Brya managed to drop her quilt block into the toilet."

"And flush it," Liz added.

"Yes, that too." Courtney laughed nervously. "I suppose she must have panicked."

Perched on the edge of the bed and intent on the computer tablet in her hands, Brya looked anything but panicked. Strewn across the lovely Rose of Sharon Room were other signs of Brya's boredom: coloring books, crayons, and several of the Gene Stratton-Porter books from the room's bookshelf.

"I read *Freckles* when I was about your age," Liz said, pointing at one of the novels. "It was my favorite book for a whole summer."

"I haven't read much of it yet," Brya admitted. "I like the swamp part. Is that swamp around here?"

Liz shook her head. "I don't think it exists anymore."

"I figured," Brya said, then returned her attention to the tablet.

Since Courtney was fidgeting near the bathroom door, Liz hurried inside to inspect the damage. The floor was surprisingly clean. "The toilet didn't overflow?"

"It did," Courtney said, "but that nice maid mopped it up before she left to find you."

Sarah to the rescue, Liz thought. Then she sighed. "I'll go get my plunger and drain snake."

By the time Liz fished the quilt block from the toilet, she had to mop the bathroom floor again. After cleaning up, she fled to the front porch for a moment of peace.

The midsummer sun shone dazzlingly bright on the white trim of the inn. The temperature climbed into the nineties, and not even a breeze off nearby Jaynes Lake could dissipate the still and heavy air. It was one of those baking summer days that smelled of hot brick and horse sweat from the Amish buggies clopping up and down the street. On Mondays, local farmers and craftsmen delivered their wares to the charming downtown shops, where tourists and locals alike snapped them up.

Liz usually enjoyed the bustle of summer, even on hot days, but she'd been slightly out of sorts lately, feeling as if a storm was brewing. To be honest, she missed Jackson Cross, the mayor of Pleasant Creek and her good friend. He'd left for a fishing trip on Saturday. Even with the activity of the inn, Liz found her thoughts turning to him often.

Liz collected the small stack of envelopes and flyers from the antique mailbox. She walked over to lean against one of the porch posts as she flipped through the mail, hoping for a letter from Steve to brighten her day.

She didn't find a letter among the bills, but she did receive a postcard inviting her to a fund-raiser dinner. The historical society was trying once again to raise money for work on the courthouse, one of the oldest buildings in Pleasant Creek. Liz wished them well in their efforts to spruce it up, though she had recently been inside the musty building and wasn't sure it needed much more than minor remodeling and a good airing out.

With that thought, Liz remembered she had jury duty coming up. She frowned. *Tomorrow. I have jury duty tomorrow, because my week cannot be any more miserable.*

"That's not a happy face."

Liz turned and spotted her dear friend Naomi Mason on the sidewalk only a few yards away. She hadn't even noticed her friend's approach. The sight of Naomi's smiling face cheered her. "How did you get away from the bakery? I know you must be busy with all the tourists in town."

"We are. In fact, I finally broke down and hired another assistant. Now I can sneak off for a few minutes. So, why do you look so unhappy?" Naomi's smile turned mischievous as she tucked her dark curls behind one ear. "Could it be because a certain furniture builder we both know is out of town?"

"I admit to missing Jackson," Liz said, "but I was remembering that I have jury duty in the morning. It isn't that I mind serving the community. I know jury duty is important, but I never actually get to serve. Lawyers never make it through the questioning process, not even boring ex-patent lawyers like me. That means I'll be sitting at the courthouse all morning for nothing."

Naomi crossed her arms over her chest. "I can see your problem. You're not looking at this right."

"I'm not?"

"The last time I had jury duty, I was thrilled. Just think about it. A whole morning of no responsibilities and no one able to call you away. I love the bakery, but sometimes a forced morning away is glorious."

"I suppose."

"Take a good book, settle in, and enjoy a few hours of downtime. Treat it like a little vacation," Naomi urged. "Oh, and be sure to bring your own coffee. The stuff in the jury lounge is vile. It was the one dark moment in a great morning the last time I served. Run by the coffee shop; your stomach lining will thank you."

Liz let Naomi's words sink in. Things had been crazy at the inn lately, and even a dull vacation might be nice. She felt a smile creep up.

Naomi pointed at it. "See? It's all in how you look at it. And the seats in the jury waiting room aren't nearly as uncomfortable as the straight-backed wooden ones scattered all over the rest of the building."

"Good. Thanks for the attitude adjustment." Liz snuck a glance at her watch and yelped. "I need to drop this mail off inside. I'm expecting another guest."

"No problem," Naomi said with a wave. "Have a good time tomorrow."

Liz had barely gotten the mail put away before her new guest arrived, carrying a plaid suitcase and a large wicker hamper. The woman appeared to be in her early forties like Liz. Her short, dark brown hair was slicked back against her head. The severe haircut didn't match the rest of the woman's look, which was heavy on layers of gauzy fabrics in Indian prints.

"Davidia Burke?" Liz asked.

"Yes." The woman set the hamper at her feet and glanced around the foyer approvingly. "This is a beautiful old place to turn into an inn."

"Thank you," Liz said. "The Olde Mansion Inn has been a bed-and-breakfast under various owners since the 1980s."

"I heard you have a wonderful quilt shop too," Davidia said.

"Yes, Sew Welcome is right through there. We'll pass by it when I show you to your room. I've booked you into the Somewhere in Time Room. I think you'll like it. May I help you with your luggage?"

"If you don't mind grabbing the suitcase, that would be great." Davidia picked up the hamper. "I'll carry Cleopatra."

Liz peered at the hamper in surprise. Although the inn allowed small pets, Davidia hadn't mentioned a dog or a cat when she booked the reservation. "Is Cleopatra a kitty? I can provide a disposable litter box if you need one." She had learned to stock a few emergency pet supplies from past experiences.

Davidia laughed. "No, Cleo isn't a kitty." She unsnapped the catch on the hamper and flipped it open. A long, bright green snake raised its head to look at Liz.

With a shriek, Liz jumped away from the hamper. Unfortunately, the back of her leg touched the sleeping bulldog, causing Beans to leap to his feet. The dog's movement made Liz's overbalance worse, and she tumbled backward over him.

Pinwheeling her arms in a vain attempt to regain her balance, Liz struck the edge of a small table where Sarah had placed a tall vase of freshly cut gladioli. The vase rocked back and forth for an instant, then turned over, dumping the flowers and water onto Liz. The vase hit the floor and shattered.

Liz picked a wet flower from her cheek. A quiet morning of jury duty had suddenly taken on a whole new appeal.

On Tuesday morning after Liz finished setting up the coffee-maker for breakfast, she passed by the staircase and discovered Brya dropping crayons from the second-floor landing. As each crayon hit the polished floor below, it left a tiny blob of wavy color. Judging from the speckles on the floor, Brya had been doing her crayon drops for a while.

Brya spotted Liz heading for the stairs and disappeared by the time Liz reached the second floor. She gathered the rest of the crayons on the floor and knocked on the door of the Rose of Sharon Room.

Courtney opened the door and smiled at Liz. "Yes?"

Liz held up the crayons. "Your daughter was dropping crayons off the landing. I would prefer she didn't do that anymore."

Courtney looked startled, then turned toward the room and beckoned to her daughter. "Were you dropping crayons off the landing?"

"I was going to color," Brya said, blinking at her mother in angelic innocence. "But crayons are so rolly. They must have rolled off."

"It was an accident," Courtney told Liz, "and I'm sure it won't happen again."

"I watched Brya drop a crayon," Liz said calmly. "It didn't roll. It was released from her hand over the railing."

Courtney stared at Liz. "Are you calling my daughter a liar?"

"I'm telling you what happened," Liz said, maintaining her level tone. "Obviously, it differs from what your daughter said. At any rate, it would be best if Brya kept her crayons in your room." As she handed over the rest of the crayons, she had a terrible image of crayon additions to the beautiful Gene Stratton-Porter prints that hung on the walls. Liz nearly snatched the crayons back, but she couldn't come up with a reason for barring crayons from the room, so she simply said a silent prayer for the survival of the prints.

"I'm sure Brya will be more careful," Courtney said, her tone making it clear that she was still offended by Liz's accusations.

Liz checked her watch. If she quickly cleaned up the floor, she still might have time to grab a cup of coffee from The Coffee Cup on the way to the courthouse. She clattered down the stairs, only to freeze in horror at the bottom. Beans stood in the middle of the fallen crayons, which had been reduced to slime-covered bits. A shard of bright green crayon hung out of his mouth as he looked up at Liz and wiggled his rear end in his version of a tail wag.

"What am I going to do with this mess?" Liz moaned.

Sarah walked through the doorway from the dining room. "Did you say something, ma'am?"

Liz pointed at the floor. "One of our guests fed Beans crayons."

Sarah's eyes widened. "I can clean the floor before anyone comes down for breakfast."

"Are you sure you'll have time after I already saddled you with serving breakfast?" Liz had whipped up cinnamon rolls for the guests, and the smell of the cooling rolls competed with the scent of chewed crayons in the stairwell.

Sarah nodded. "Cleaning up will only take me a few minutes."

"I wonder how many crayons Beans swallowed," Liz said. "Do you think they're toxic?"

"I would imagine not," Sarah answered as she knelt and began picking up slobbery fragments. "They are just colored wax."

"Right, good thinking." Liz fished the rest of the crayon from Beans's mouth, along with more slobber. As she did so, she caught sight of the dog's teeth, which looked like pointy bits of rainbow.

Since Sarah had both floor cleanup and breakfast to handle, Liz was stuck with dental hygiene duty for Beans. As she used the dog's toothbrush to scrub wavy rainbows away, she had a wry thought about the glamour of being an innkeeper.

When Liz finally rushed out the door, she was running very late. In order to reach the courthouse in time, she couldn't grab a café mocha from The Coffee Cup, no matter how desperately she felt like she needed it. *I sure hope Naomi was exaggerating the poor quality of courthouse coffee.*

The entrance at the rear of the courthouse where the jury duty notice had directed her to enter was little used by the public, and the town was clearly taking advantage of that to cut costs. When Liz pushed through the glass doors, she saw that the small, dark foyer was completely empty of decoration or furniture, and there were deep shadows in the corners. The space resembled a low-budget movie set.

To the left of the doors, two security guards clutched foam cups of coffee and leaned against a table, waiting to scan the bags of everyone who entered the courthouse.

"Jury duty?" one guard asked, heaving himself away from the table.

Liz nodded.

The guard added, "You're almost late. You might be the last one through. Please place your belongings on the belt."

Liz dropped her tote bag on the short conveyor belt that carried it into a smaller version of the X-ray machines at the airport. Liz glanced at the image on the screen. The ghostly jumble of odd-shaped edges and points appeared mildly alarming. When the tote bag came out on the other side of the machine, the second guard poked in it briefly with the end of her baton.

The first guard ushered Liz to the metal detector. "Do you have anything metal on your person?" His tone was so indifferent that it barely sounded like a question.

"No."

"Step through, please."

She walked through the metal detector, which remained blissfully silent. Liz knew courtroom rules inside and out, but she still found herself relieved when she was waved on. Irrational as it sounded, there was something about security searches that made her feel vaguely guilty.

"Take the elevator to the fourth floor. Turn left when the door opens," the guard called after her in a tone that suggested he'd given the exact same directions countless times.

"Thanks," she said over her shoulder.

Upstairs, Liz followed small signs through a twisting series of identical beige halls to reach the jury waiting room. On this floor, the marble trim so abundant below was replaced with textured wallpaper. The industrial carpet with a blue-gray herringbone pattern was probably chosen to hide dirt, but it did little to hide the wear pattern from years of foot traffic.

Like all the other jury waiting rooms Liz had ever seen, this one resembled a tiny movie theater with rows of connected seats facing a large television. On the screen, a blonde morning-show host danced her way to her seat.

Near the propped-open door where Liz stood, little empty space remained. A round table occupied most of the area, and several hard-backed chairs, which Liz knew from experience were painful seating, surrounded it.

The only other furniture was a podium where the jury clerk, a plain woman in her fifties, with her dark blonde hair pulled into a tight bun, hardly looked at Liz as she signed her in and handed her a blue *Juror* sticker. Liz waited for the standard lecture about not wandering around the halls, but the jury clerk stared down at the list in front of her without saying anything.

Liz searched the theater-style seats, trying to choose the best reading spot. The potential jurors who had arrived earlier had chosen their seats with optimum empty space around them, and Liz didn't want to encroach on anyone else's privacy. She had no more urge for aimless small talk than they did.

She didn't even consider the table and chairs. Not only did she know that the chairs were uncomfortable, but she could already tell it was the social zone for the room. The people in the seats were squirming to find a more comfortable position while chatting, or more accurately, while listening. A heavily made-up woman with big, highlighted hair dominated the conversation. She talked loudly and waved her hands, which made her long nails flash in the overhead lights.

Mildly surprised that she didn't recognize a single face in the room, Liz walked down the side aisle to the front of the theater-style seats and found an empty one. The brownish-burgundy upholstery was padded enough to be quite comfortable. She hoped she would be able to read despite the loud social area nearby. Liz rooted in her bag and pulled out the mystery novel she'd snagged from the inn's library. She was looking forward to losing herself in the whodunit.

Unfortunately, the queen bee of the social group seemed to grow louder and louder with each passing minute. She regaled her audience, both the ones who'd chosen the role and those trying desperately to block her out, with horror stories of how terribly mistreated she was by nearly everyone she'd ever met. Apparently, she was in a financial war with her cheap ex-husband, who was attempting to trick her out of something that was hers for the sake of his evil fiancée. From that topic, she ranted about the shyster lawyer who had represented her husband in the divorce, thereby cheating her out of her due.

Fifteen minutes ticked by. The large clock on the wall showed Liz exactly how long she'd not been able to read her book. With her annoyance growing, she felt increasingly sorry for the poor man who'd been married to such a drama queen.

Liz turned to the social group, wondering if they were getting tired of the woman's tirade. Judging by their body language, several seemed to be trying to disconnect from the conversation. They had pushed their chairs away from the table until they were nearly touching the walls. Two even rocked back on the rear legs of their chairs, putting an extra inch or two between them and the complaining woman.

"You wouldn't believe what my eye doctor told me yesterday," the woman half shouted.

Ah, a new topic, Liz thought, settling into her new twisted position where she could watch the woman. *Someone at her table will certainly shush her soon.*

"He said I needed glasses. Me. I'm too young for glasses. But he told me if I didn't get them, I'd fail my next driving test." The woman crossed her arms over her chest and scowled. "I bet the BMV workers are in the pocket of the eyeglass hucksters. They probably get a kickback for every person they force to buy glasses."

That's one of the most ridiculous things I've ever heard, Liz thought. She felt her annoyance at the noisy woman continue to increase, causing the muscles in her neck and shoulders to tense.

"This whole area is a sewer," the woman insisted. "It's because of that crazy cult outside of town."

Cult? Liz hadn't heard about any cults operating in Pleasant Creek. Not that she knew much about cults. She mostly associated them with drinking poisoned kiddie beverages or worshiping snakes.

"I actually grew up in that cult," the woman said, "but I wasn't going to live under the thumb of elders like Nathan Manz."

Liz gasped. Nathan Manz was the bishop of the Amish community and someone her own Amish relatives and friends held in high regard. He certainly wasn't a cultist. Liz couldn't believe the woman was calling the Amish a cult. She glanced around the room and saw that a number of people had turned in their chairs at the vicious slight and were shooting outraged looks toward the social area.

Liz searched for the jury clerk. Certainly, she could quiet the woman. But the podium was empty, and the clerk was nowhere to be seen. She scanned the crowd again, noting the angry faces. If someone didn't say something to quiet the woman, Liz feared things might turn ugly.

She stood and slipped her tote bag onto her shoulder but held her book, intending to use it for a prop. Then she squared her shoulders, a trick that always made her feel a little more confident. One of her law school professors had once told her that if you try to *look* confident, your feelings would eventually catch up.

Liz walked down the aisle to the table and stood next to the woman, waiting for her to stop talking. Clearly, she was giving the woman more credit than was deserved.

"Can you imagine living your whole life in frumpy clothes and prayer bonnets?" The woman burst out laughing. "It was like being raised by American settlers."

Giving up on the hope that the self-absorbed woman would notice her, Liz eventually said, "Excuse me."

The woman spun in her chair. She gave Liz a long, appraising look, her gaze lingering on Liz's Saint Laurent tote, a holdover from her attorney days. "Yes?"

"I was hoping you might speak a little more quietly to your group here." Liz held up her book. "A number of us are reading to pass the time, and it would be easier if the room was a bit quieter."

"You think I'm loud?" the woman demanded as she stood, putting her well within Liz's personal space.

Liz didn't back up, though she knew that was what the woman had intended. Instead, she studied the woman's irate face and noted that the heavy makeup couldn't obscure the lines around her eyes and mouth. She wasn't as young as her clothes and hairstyle had implied. "I think you're speaking louder than the situation requires."

"I disagree."

The leash Liz had on her temper began to fray. "I don't doubt that, but the reality is that many of us are trying to read. And most of us are not interested in your ill-informed opinions of the Amish community."

The woman leaned still closer to Liz and shouted, "My opinions are anything but ill-informed! I was raised by those monsters. And they were exactly like you. They thought they were better than me too. They thought I should shut up. But you know what? I'm not shutting up. I'm going to exercise my freedom of speech as an American citizen."

Liz rolled her eyes. "This is hardly a free-speech issue."

"No, it's a nosy-parker issue. You best mind your own business and take your seat if you know what's good for you." The woman's face reddened, and she clenched her fists.

Liz honestly believed the obnoxious woman might strike her. "Fine." She held up a hand and took a step back. "But other people in this room are tired of you too. Don't be surprised if I'm not the only one you have to deal with."

The woman waved her off. "I'm scared to death."

Liz needed some space before she ended up starting a fight. As she headed to the lounge, she dropped her book into her bag and thought about Naomi's suggestion to treat jury duty like a little vacation.

"Worst vacation ever," she muttered.

3

The jury lounge was neither luxurious nor spacious. A pay phone hung on the wall, and Liz thought about how rare they were becoming in a country full of cell phones. Were there really still people who weren't connected to the world by a device in their pocket?

Near the phone a battered walnut table held a coffeemaker; the carafe was mostly full. She saw doors to restrooms and another door that led to the jury clerk's office. Since Liz had noticed a door to that office out in the hall, she assumed it had two entrances. She wondered if she should go in and ask the clerk to do something about the loud woman. Liz tapped her foot nervously as she considered it but decided that she wasn't here to make waves. She was going to be in the courthouse for only a couple of hours, and she could always use the lounge as a refuge.

Liz poured herself a cup of coffee, adding cream and sugar, then winced at the slightly gray color the coffee turned in her foam cup. It wasn't an encouraging sign of tasty things to come. She carried the cup over to a small upholstered chair and sat down. She could still hear the woman in the next room, but she wasn't nearly as loud. Here, Liz thought she could probably read.

She opened her book, then paused to look around the room. It wasn't exactly a place she'd pick for a short vacation from the inn. Like the hallways and the jury waiting room, the walls in the lounge were relentlessly beige, though the textured wallpaper was missing. This beige came from glossy paint that highlighted the imperfections in the old walls. The floor was gray tile, probably for easy cleanup. A tiny television hung on the wall. The sound was muted, and the screen showed the local weather.

Liz was a little surprised that she had the lounge all to herself. She had expected some of the other jurors to slip away to escape the noise, but she certainly wasn't going to complain about the solitude. She turned her gaze toward her book while she took her first sip of the coffee and nearly choked. Sputtering, she looked down at the gray-brown brew. Naomi had not exaggerated the vileness of the flavor. Hoping more sugar or creamer would help, Liz returned to the table and began spooning things into her cup.

The obnoxious woman's voice seemed to be getting even louder. When two people walked through the doorway from the waiting room, Liz tensed up, anticipating a repeat of the earlier confrontation.

The loud woman merely gave Liz a nasty look and gestured toward the coffeepot. "You done?"

"Be my guest," Liz said, half-hoping the woman choked on the terrible stuff in the pot. She turned to head back to her seat, only to be bumped hard, sending a shower of coffee onto the gray tile.

The loud woman smirked at her. "Excuse you."

What, are we in grade school? Liz rolled her eyes and walked to her chair, pointedly opening her book as she sat down.

The loud woman and her companion took their cups of coffee and left.

Liz sighed in relief. Maybe she could read a few pages before it was time to watch the movie, the one where they heard all about how jury duty was both essential and rewarding.

In her mystery novel, the amateur detective seemed to get an amazing number of clues from her cat, making Liz grumble, "That's the kind of pet I need. How come no one in these books ends up with a dog who eats crayons and naps like it's his job?"

Two more people entered the lounge, one leaning heavily on a cane. Liz felt her face flush and wondered if they'd heard her talking to herself. If they did, neither showed any sign of it.

The older man whispered loudly to his companion, "If that woman doesn't shut up, there's going to be a murder right there in the jury room."

The other man chuckled. "I'm not sure you should make murder jokes in a courthouse."

"Who says I'm joking?" The older man stared down at the coffeepot. "Do you think this is any good?"

"It's horrible," Liz volunteered.

The man nodded. "I was afraid of that. I shouldn't be drinking it anyway." He squinted at Liz. "You're the one who tried to shut that harpy up, aren't you?"

"I did speak to her."

"Thanks for trying," the older man said. "Though I was hoping you'd punch her."

Liz's eyes widened in alarm. "I certainly wouldn't have hit her."

The man grunted. "Too bad. I'm considering tripping her with my cane if I get the chance."

The younger man laughed. "If you do, I promise to swear it looked like an accident to me."

"She does seem to be trying everyone's patience," Liz said quietly.

"I didn't like what she said about the Amish," the older man responded. "I dated a young Amish girl once during her *Rumschpringe*. She was lovely and kind. It broke my heart when she went back to the community." He sighed deeply.

"I never dated anyone Amish," the other man said, "but I work with a few at Cross Furniture. They're great guys."

Liz's ears perked up. Even just hearing the name of the business that Jackson owned made her miss him more. "Cross Furniture looks like a good place to work."

"It is."

Liz checked the clock on the wall. "It's probably about time for the movie."

The older man harrumphed. "I'd hate to miss that. It may have changed from the other three times I've sat through it."

"Have you ever actually served on a jury during a trial?" Liz asked.

"Once," the man said. "It isn't as interesting as it seems on TV."

"So few things are," his companion said.

Liz walked into the waiting room but paused before sitting down again, choosing instead to stand not far from the jury lounge doorway. She noticed a number of people shooting irritated looks toward the still noisy social area. Once the film began, it should offer everyone a short break.

"If this trial has anything to do with those Amish cultists, I'm sure I'll be excused from the jury right away," the noisy woman crowed. "No lawyer would risk me being on a jury with what I know about those people. I'm aware of what they're *really* like."

"Quiet and unassuming?" the older man from the break room asked.

The woman pointed at him. "That's what they *want* you to think."

The man crossed his arms over his chest. "Then they should all be very happy, because it is what I think."

The woman snorted and turned her back on him, then launched into more snarky remarks to those at the table.

Liz found the woman's attitude sickening and hoped the jury clerk would return and at least force the room to be quiet for the movie. They could all use a break from the hateful tirade before the simmering anger broke out into something unfortunate. Once more, she scanned the annoyed faces of the other jurors. But one woman, seated not far from the social area, didn't appear just annoyed. She was furious. The phrase *if looks could kill* popped into Liz's mind.

Liz realized that the obnoxious woman had changed her topic while Liz was distracted. Now she was making unpleasant remarks about Liz herself. "She must be one of those Amish lovers." The woman snickered. "Like the old man over there."

Liz took a seat and carefully smoothed the front of her pale blue skirt while counting to ten slowly in her head. Once she was completely calm, she intended to go find the jury clerk and insist upon some action. It was time to put a stop to the abusive woman's diatribe. She hit ten and started to rise.

At the same moment the jury clerk stepped into the room from the lounge, stopped in front of the TV screen, and announced, "Thank you all for coming to serve your community as jurors today. The case for which you were called has ended in a plea bargain, and your presence will no longer be required. You can consider your obligation fulfilled, and you may all go home. If you are self-employed and need the form for reimbursement, please stop by my office."

Relieved to be released, Liz nearly rocketed from her seat, knocking her tote bag to the floor in the process. She knelt awkwardly and shoveled her belongings back into the bag. Then she realized her book wasn't there. She stood and looked on her seat and the seat beside hers. Where had the book gone?

She went to the jury lounge and spotted the book on the floor beside the chair where she'd been sitting. When she thought she'd shoved the book into the bag, she must have actually dropped it onto the floor. She carefully slipped the book into the bag, then returned to the waiting room. It was completely empty.

The hallway was empty as well, and Liz chuckled. Obviously, she hadn't been the only person eager to leave. She pushed the elevator button and waited, listening to the mechanism groan as the car rode up to the fourth floor.

The elevator door opened, revealing the obnoxious woman from the jury room. Her face was distorted with swelling that had turned her eyes into mere slits, and her lips were tinted blue despite the lipstick partially smeared across her cheeks.

The woman staggered out of the elevator and grabbed at Liz desperately. Wheezing, she clutched Liz's arms. Then her knees buckled, and she collapsed to the floor.

4

In the empty courthouse hallway, Liz dropped to her knees beside the collapsed woman. "Can you hear me?" she asked.

The woman clawed at her own throat, and Liz realized she was struggling to breathe, but Liz didn't know what was wrong or what she could do to help. She turned toward the office doors and shouted, "Help! Someone help!"

The woman's breathing sounded like a shrill whistle.

Liz caught the woman's swollen hand and noticed her lips were moving. Liz leaned close to her face.

"She tried to kill me."

"She who?" Liz asked, but if the woman answered, the sound was drowned out as people rushed from the offices all around and started babbling in the hallway.

Liz yelled to the crowd, "Someone call 911!"

Turning once again to the collapsed woman, Liz saw that she was now unconscious. Liz could hardly detect the woman's breath. She tilted the woman's head back and began mouth-to-mouth resuscitation in the hope that assisting the woman to breathe would keep her alive until real help arrived.

The elevator next to Liz *dinged*, and two security guards hurried out. They dropped to the floor next to Liz. "Let us take over," one guard said. "We're trained."

Liz gladly handed over the job and went to stand next to the jury clerk.

The clerk was wringing her hands as she stared at the sick woman's swollen face. "What's wrong with her?" she asked.

Liz shook her head. "I'm not sure. Do you know if anyone called for an ambulance?"

The woman nodded but didn't say anything else.

While one of the guards administered CPR, the other grabbed the woman's purse and dumped it out. A long, slender tube that Liz couldn't identify bounced out with the other items. "She's got an EpiPen. This is anaphylaxis." The guard popped the end off the tube and slammed it into the unconscious woman's thigh.

Almost instantly, the woman on the floor began to breathe better, though her breathing remained wheezy. The other guard stopped resuscitation efforts but propped the woman up to help her breathe.

The guard who had administered the shot picked up the purse again and went through the woman's wallet and pulled out an ID. "Ms. Wexler," he called loudly into the woman's face. "Nora, can you hear me?"

Nora Wexler turned to face him, though Liz wondered how much she could possibly see through the slits of her swollen eyes. It must have been enough because the sick woman nodded. Then she glanced around the room frantically. She finally settled her gaze in Liz's general direction. She raised a swollen hand and wheezed, "She tried to kill me."

Everyone looked at Liz.

"I found her in the elevator," Liz explained, "and I was trying to help her."

"You were fighting with her in the waiting room," the jury clerk said, backing away from Liz. "One of the other jurors reported it."

"I was *fighting* with her?" Liz stared at the woman in shock. "No. All I did was ask her to speak more quietly so people could read. She's the one who was yelling at me."

"Now isn't the time for this," one of the guards snapped. "Ms. Wexler is in the middle of an allergic reaction, which is restricting her oxygen and causing her to be disoriented and confused. We don't need to make the situation even worse."

The elevator *dinged* again, and Liz was relieved to see EMTs lugging equipment with them. They asked everyone to clear enough space for them to work.

Liz was eager to comply. She'd had enough of her jury duty vacation for one day.

When Liz arrived at the Olde Mansion Inn, she immediately ducked into Sew Welcome. She needed to process the weird morning with people she trusted, and there were few people in the world that Liz trusted more than the owners of the quilt shop.

Mary Ann Berne looked up from where she was waiting on Harriet and caught sight of Liz. As always, Liz's friend was perfectly put together with a lovely silver-gray short-sleeved sweater that matched her hair almost exactly. Mary Ann gave Liz a barely perceptible nod, then smiled at her. Mary Ann's gentle, welcoming smile made Liz feel better already.

Liz started across the room, but Mary Ann's business partner, Sadie Schwarzentruber, caught Liz by the arm and tugged her toward the airy workroom, holding a finger to her lips. Since Sadie was rarely quiet, Liz followed without comment until they were out of sight of the counter.

"You don't want Harriet to see you," Sadie whispered. "She had another dream, and you look like you really don't need to hear it."

Liz stifled a moan. "You're right. After the morning I experienced, I don't have the energy for any more dreams."

"You sit," Sadie ordered. "I'll snag you a cup of coffee, and then you can tell me all about it."

Liz almost laughed. If there was one thing Sadie loved, it was hearing about other people. "Thank you," she said sincerely. "The coffee at the courthouse was terrible."

Sadie patted her arm and rushed out of the shop.

Liz collapsed in one of the comfortable chairs that surrounded the worktable. She gazed out the tall windows, drinking in the calming sight of a beautiful coal-black horse pulling a black Amish buggy down the street in front of the inn.

The horse and buggy reminded her of Nora Wexler's hateful remarks in the jury waiting room. *How can anyone detest the Amish? They're such peaceful people.* Liz knew from past experience that not everyone viewed the Amish as she did, and she understood that the Amish weren't perfect any more than anyone else. But she still couldn't comprehend the pure animosity that Nora had spouted at the courthouse.

She turned sharply at the sound of footsteps on the wood floor.

Mary Ann stood in the workroom entryway. The silky hair of her long bob perfectly framed her sweet face. "The coast is clear. I saw Sadie stow you in here."

"Harriet means well, and I'll be happy to listen to her dream experience later." Liz sighed. "But I really don't have the energy right now."

Mary Ann's expression grew puzzled. "You sound like you had a tough morning. When I've had jury duty, it was mostly boring."

"This was anything but," Liz said. "A woman almost died of some kind of allergic reaction, and she blamed me for it, which I don't understand at all. I tried to help her."

"I have a cousin who is allergic to shellfish," Mary Ann said. "I saw her have a severe reaction once. It was terrifying for her. That kind of fear can be disorienting, I'm sure."

Liz nodded. "You're probably right. That's what the security guard said too. But I did have words with the woman before she got sick. She was being obnoxiously loud, and I barely read a page or two of my novel the whole time I was there." She winced at her own words. "Which sounds quite petty now in light of how awful the allergic reaction must have been for the poor woman."

A harrumph in the doorway heralded Sadie's return with a tray of coffee mugs. She passed one to Liz, who immediately took a long, soothing sip. Sadie handed another to Mary Ann, then sat down with her own mug and pointed at Liz. "If you had words with the woman, she deserved it." She smiled a little. "Not that I personally have room to call anyone out for being loud."

"It was totally different. You're nothing like this woman," Liz responded. "She said horrible things about the Amish, and she practically threatened me for asking her to keep the volume down."

"Then I rest my case," Sadie said. "What goes around comes around."

"She deserved being scolded, maybe," Liz admitted. "But no one deserves to be so sick. She almost stopped breathing before a security guard discovered that she had an injector for the allergy in her purse."

"My cousin has one of those," Mary Ann said. "Though they don't always work. The symptoms can come back. I do hope the poor woman is all right."

"I'm sure she'll be fine. They're very good at the hospital," Sadie said dismissively, then turned to Liz. "Now I have a big question. Did I hear Sarah say you let someone check in with a snake?"

Mary Ann's eyes widened. "Please tell me you didn't."

Liz shrugged. "It fits the weight limit for pets in our printed rules. It never occurred to me that someone would haul a snake to the inn, but I could sense the woman would make an issue of it if I refused. I did insist that the snake stay locked up the whole time it's here. And I'll definitely be revising the pet rules on our website."

"You'll forgive me if I don't go upstairs while it's here." Mary Ann shuddered. "You tell me when she finally checks out. By the way, which person was it? I know it's not Harriet. She would certainly have told us all about it."

"The snake is owned by Davidia Burke," Liz answered.

"Oh, I met her. She bought quite a bit at the shop yesterday," Mary Ann said. "She seems like such a nice person. Not at all snaky."

Liz laughed. "Well, technically, I own a dog. Do I seem doggy?"

"No, but Beans was inherited when you bought the inn," Sadie reminded her. "I'm not sure that counts."

Liz took another long sip from her mug, and again her thoughts turned to Nora and the horrifying sight of her swollen face.

Mary Ann reached out and patted Liz's arm. "Try not to worry too much about the sick woman."

Surprised as always by Mary Ann's uncanny ability to read people, Liz nodded. "I think it's a mix of worry and guilt."

"You know, it's been my experience that when people are really unpleasant and loud, it's because they want someone to listen to them and care." Mary Ann set her coffee mug on the table. "I wonder if I should bake a pie for the woman. Of course, I'd need to know what she's allergic to."

"They may not have kept her at the hospital," Sadie said. "Don't allergic reactions resolve fairly quickly? You could end up wandering the hospital halls looking for someone in need of a pie."

Mary Ann raised her eyebrows. "I can think of worse ways to spend my time."

"You have a good heart," Liz said. "But since we're speaking of time, it's time I get back to work. Sarah doesn't even know I'm here. I snuck in."

"Sneak in here anytime." Sadie smiled. "We're always glad to hide you."

"And you know I appreciate it," Liz replied. She carried her mug out of the shop and stopped at the sound of raised voices. She followed the voices to the sitting room where Sarah stood with a dust rag in her hand, facing Davidia.

"Is something wrong?" Liz asked.

The look of relief on Sarah's face was almost comical. "Miss Burke has lost her pet."

Liz turned to Davidia in alarm and spoke in a harried whisper. "Your snake is loose? How did that happen? You promised me that you'd keep the snake's hamper latched."

"I did," Davidia said. "Even though Cleopatra normally likes a certain amount of freedom, but I was as good as my word. I checked on

Cleo before I went down to breakfast. She was curled up on her warm rock. I have a special battery-operated rock for travel, but it doesn't get quite as warm as the electric rock at home. And it runs through batteries like you wouldn't believe."

"I'm sure it does," Liz said. "So you looked at the snake this morning and left the hamper unlatched?"

"I most certainly did *not* leave the hamper unlatched," Davidia huffed. "After breakfast I returned to my room and started working on my quilt. I'm using a Monkey Wrench quilt block pattern. I like the way it resembles two snakes kissing."

The comparison distracted Liz for a moment, and she realized that she was never going to be able to look at that pattern again without seeing kissing snakes.

Davidia showed no sign of noticing the shudder that went through Liz. "I bought some beautiful green fabrics at Sew Welcome yesterday that work perfectly to bring the idea across even more clearly."

Liz tried to direct the conversation back to the important topic at hand. "And your snake?"

"I noticed that Cleo was being awfully quiet in her hamper. She's really quite a lively companion as long as she hasn't eaten recently. I peeked into the basket to see what she was doing. She was missing." Davidia's voice cracked. "I had to undo the latch to look inside, so I know she didn't leave on her own."

"Then how did the snake get out of the hamper?" Liz asked.

"The answer is obvious," Davidia said. "You have a snake-napper in this inn."

After calming the distraught woman as much as possible, Liz and Sarah began searching the inn for the missing snake. "Just tell people that you're looking for a small pet," Liz suggested. "Don't say snake."

"Yes, ma'am," Sarah said. "But what if someone asks what kind of pet? I don't like to lie. It is an offense against *Gött*."

"Right," Liz said. "Do you have an Amish word for *snake*?"

"*Schlange*. If it is not poisonous."

"It isn't. So if anyone asks what kind of pet it is, simply tell them it's a Schlange. Then you're telling the truth. And if they have more questions, tell them to ask me. Will that be all right?"

"*Ja*," Sarah said. "I can do that."

Sarah and Liz rushed upstairs on the assumption that it was unlikely anyone would miss seeing the snake slithering down the stairs. Liz knocked on doors and told guests about a missing small pet, asking if they'd seen any animals. At each room, they received variations on the same answer.

"The only animal I've seen is the bulldog downstairs," Courtney said, holding the door open only a crack. The cool tone of her voice suggested she was still upset with Liz about the crayon incident.

Brya poked her head into the space beside her mother. "And the dog is boring."

Courtney frowned at her daughter. "That's not very nice."

"Sorry," Brya mumbled.

"That's all right," Liz told her. "It's really kind of true. Though I wouldn't want him to get sick or hurt just the same. He chewed up those crayons you dropped this morning."

Brya looked at Liz in dismay. "Is he okay?"

Courtney shushed her daughter and turned to Liz. "Enough about the crayons. There are no stray pets in here." Then she closed the door in Liz's face.

Liz sighed. It was nice to see the little girl had some conscience, but the exchange brought her no closer to finding the snake.

When the second floor was thoroughly checked, Sarah searched the third floor. No one was booked into either of the third-floor rooms, and with the inn being air-conditioned, the snake might head up to the unfinished storage area on the top floor where it would be the warmest. But Sarah turned up nothing crawly at all.

Beginning to feel desperate, Liz dashed downstairs to investigate the first-floor rooms, especially the kitchen, which might retain some warmth from the stove and could be alluring to a snake.

When she heard a loud knock on the back door in the utility room, she was on her hands and knees, flashing a light in the narrow space between the fridge and the cabinet and marveling at how clean it was. *I'm beginning to think Sarah might actually be magic.* The young Amish woman did more cleaning in her part-time hours than Liz would have been able to manage if she did nothing else all day.

After scrambling to her feet, Liz dusted off her knees and the hem of her skirt, more from habit than any belief that she could have picked up dirt in the immaculate kitchen. She rushed into the utility room and spotted Stan Houghton, Pleasant Creek's chief of police, standing outside. She threw open the door. "Please tell me you've come by for coffee and a leftover cinnamon roll."

The stocky, gray-haired man smiled as he stepped through the door and patted his ample stomach. "I wouldn't say no to the coffee and cinnamon roll, but I came by to talk to you about the excitement at the courthouse this morning."

"You mean the woman who got so sick? Nora Wexler?" Liz said. "I hope she's all right."

Chief Houghton shook his head. "I'm afraid not. Nora Wexler

died. She was allergic to beestings. The doctor found two stings on her arm, very close to one another. For someone with a severe allergy, that's too much venom. Even with medical attention, her allergic reaction got worse and the doctors weren't able to get it under control. I understand that's rare, but it does happen."

"How horrible," Liz said. Then she cocked her head. "How on earth did she get stung twice in the courthouse? It's not exactly a garden in there."

"I wondered the same thing. Did you happen to see any bees in the elevator or the hallway?" he asked as he followed Liz to the kitchen.

Liz walked to the coffeemaker. "No. Not that I would have noticed." She paused with the carafe in her hand. "But I do remember a little garden area with flowers and benches next to the courthouse. Could she have gone there and been stung, then run to the courthouse for help?" Even as she said it, she doubted Nora would have had enough time to do that.

"Security would have seen her leave and reenter," the chief pointed out, "and they would have dealt with the medical crisis downstairs. There would have been no reason to go back upstairs. According to the doctors, the reaction began immediately, so Ms. Wexler would have been hard to miss coming into the building. You were apparently the first person to see her after she was stung."

"Well, if there were multiple bees in the elevator, I certainly didn't see them." Liz poured coffee into a thick blue mug and handed it to the chief. "Though my attention was on the swollen, gasping woman who practically fell on top of me."

"We searched the elevator and the upstairs floors and didn't find any bees. I've called in an exterminator to make a more thorough search. Some insects build nests in the walls of old buildings, and the courthouse would definitely count as an old building." Chief Houghton took a sip of his coffee. "Didn't you say something about a cinnamon roll too?"

"Of course." Liz quickly slid one of the leftover cinnamon rolls onto a china plate and handed it to him, along with a fork. "As much as I appreciate having you visit and learning what happened to that woman, I'm at a loss for what your official function is here."

Chief Houghton stuffed a bite of cinnamon roll into his mouth and sighed appreciatively. Finally, he said, "This is fantastic. Too many people put raisins in these rolls. I never liked that. When I was a kid, I always imagined bugs had crawled into my breakfast when I bit into one."

"You had a charming imagination as a child," Liz said as she crossed her arms over her chest. "But my question about your visit still stands."

The chief set his fork down on the plate. "Until we find a bee, any bee, in the courthouse, Nora Wexler's death is considered suspicious. And that means I'm chatting with everyone who had contact with her at the courthouse. I imagine it will turn out to be a waste of time, but I like getting out of the office now and then."

Liz knew the police chief was very good at friendly banter, which could be completely disarming right up until he revealed how sharply intelligent he really was. As a result, she rather doubted he was quite so disinterested in Nora's death as he seemed. "How can I help?"

"I heard you had a violent confrontation with Ms. Wexler in the jury waiting room."

Liz stared at him in shock. "Violent confrontation? Hardly. I asked her to speak more quietly so the rest of us in the room could read. She began yelling at me about first amendment rights, so I went to the jury lounge to find a more peaceful spot."

Chief Houghton took another bite of his cinnamon roll. Again Liz had to wait for his next response. "I'm not surprised someone blew it out of proportion. You would be amazed at how many times witnesses do that in their statements. Witnesses love drama, so they'll invent it out of almost anything."

Liz didn't know what to say. She was still wondering if the chief considered her an actual suspect. "I don't suppose you'd tell me who said I was violent."

He shrugged. "I can't really share the details of an investigation."

"An investigation of a beesting."

"I also have multiple reports that Ms. Wexler pointed right at you and accused you of harming her," the chief stated.

And the trap snaps, Liz thought. "She did point generally in my direction, but she was also very sick and her eyes were so swollen that I'm surprised she could even see. I don't know what prompted the accusation, but all I did was try to save her when she staggered out of the elevator."

Chief Houghton poked at the cinnamon roll. "It's a good thing you were there since everyone else had already left. Otherwise, who knows how long it would have taken for someone to find her. Why *were* you the last person to leave the jury waiting room?"

Liz didn't appreciate the direction the conversation was going and seriously considered snatching the plate out of the chief's hands. "I had dropped my book in the jury lounge, and I noticed it was missing when I gathered my things to leave. While I went back to look for it, everyone cleared out. I'm not surprised I was the last one. When the jury clerk announced that we could leave, the group acted like little kids hearing the last bell at school. I can't believe no one was trampled. Did you find out who Nora rode down in the elevator with?"

"No one remembers her on the elevator. And since she'd mixed it up with you earlier, I thought perhaps she'd come looking to talk more to you."

Liz barely resisted rolling her eyes. "I didn't see her between the time we were released and the moment she stumbled out of the elevator. If someone was involved in her allergic reaction, it wasn't me."

Chief Houghton finished the last small bite of the cinnamon roll and rinsed the plate at the sink. "The doctors at the hospital told me that Ms. Wexler *might* have been hallucinating from the lack of oxygen to her brain." He turned around to look at Liz. "Like I said, I doubt anything will come from my asking questions. Nora Wexler was stung by bees, and I can hardly arrest bees." Then he smiled. "Though I'm thinking the investigation is going really well so far because I just had a delicious cinnamon roll and some excellent coffee."

After Chief Houghton thanked her for her time and for breakfast, Liz ushered him to the door.

She watched him amble to his car, waving as if they'd parted on the best of terms. But she couldn't help wondering why she didn't feel like the matter was nearly as simple as the chief insisted.

6

After the police chief's appearance, Liz continued her secret snake hunt. Finally, she had to admit defeat. She simply couldn't find the creature. Liz became increasingly jumpy and tense, anticipating the screams of one of the guests if they ran across the snake, but no one had spotted the slithering escapee yet.

Liz walked into Sew Welcome and filled in Sadie and Mary Ann on Nora's death.

Tears glistened in Mary Ann's dark brown eyes. "I'm so sorry to hear that. I always feel particularly sad for people who were clearly unhappy."

"You're a gigantic softy," Sadie said to her friend, then looked at Liz shrewdly. "It seems odd that the chief of police would pop by to update you on some woman's accidental death."

"They can't find any bees," Liz said, "and someone told him I'd had a violent altercation with the woman."

Mary Ann shook her head. "Chief Houghton would know better than to believe that."

"I would certainly hope so," Sadie said loyally, "but he probably figured he had to investigate." Then she laughed. "What did he think? That you pulled bees out of your purse and smacked her with them?"

"That would seem unlikely," Liz replied. "I have to admit, I find it unnerving whenever I'm questioned that way."

"If you don't mind my changing the subject," Mary Ann said quietly, "what exactly is this missing pet you've been looking for? I thought there was only one guest with a pet staying with us right now, and I'd really, really like you to tell me that pet isn't loose in the inn."

Liz sighed. "I wish I could tell you that."

Mary Ann appeared startled, and she whispered, "The snake?"

Liz nodded.

"Did you find it yet?" Mary Ann squeaked.

"No, but I'm sure we will soon. You know Sarah; there's no crack or crevice in this inn that she doesn't know about and clean regularly." Liz spoke with an optimism she didn't exactly feel.

That optimism didn't grow throughout the day. During the afternoon coffee hour, Liz almost tossed her cards on the table and admitted there was a snake loose in the inn, but the image of all her guests packing their bags and leaving kept her mouth shut. Plus, Davidia skipped the social event, so at least Liz didn't have the guilt of seeing her fret about her lost pet.

Later when Liz headed for bed, she found herself nervously searching her dark rooms. Finally, she dragged Beans into her quarters, hoping the dog would sniff out the snake if it tried to get inside.

Either the snake wasn't in her rooms or Beans didn't care. He waddled to the braided rug in her living room, flopped down, and resumed the nap she'd interrupted.

Liz entered her bedroom and caught sight of her tote bag on the chair near her bed. She knew she should empty it and put it away in the closet, but she was profoundly tired and desperate for bed. Then she remembered something her mother used to say: "A task put off is a job doubled."

So Liz retrieved the tote bag and dumped its contents onto her bed to sort through. Something caught the light from the nearby lamp and glinted. *What is that?* She pushed aside a wadded-up tissue and a tube of lip balm, expecting to find a crumpled foil gum wrapper or a similar shiny object. Instead, she found a bright green crystal. She held up the small, faceted stone to the light where it sparkled beautifully.

Liz frowned. She didn't have any decorative crystals on the tote bag or her wallet either. She hadn't been wearing any jewelry with gemstones. So where had the little green crystal come from? She stared at it for a while, turning it over and over in her hand, then decided she didn't care enough to stay awake any longer.

"I must have picked it up somewhere," Liz muttered. "Maybe the last time I used this tote." *And maybe I'm getting forgetful.*

On that depressing note, Liz decided to worry about it in the morning. She put the crystal into a tiny china box on her dresser and went to bed.

The next morning Liz slipped the green crystal into her shirt pocket before she headed to the kitchen to prepare breakfast. She hummed softly under her breath as she beat eggs for frittata cups to go with locally grown melon and warm blueberry muffins for her guests. She snipped sprigs of rosemary and parsley from her herb garden outside to bring a fresh taste to the eggs. Everything went together well, and Liz patted her shirt pocket. "Maybe you'll be my lucky charm today."

When she finally sat down at the table with her guests, she immediately spotted the worried look on Davidia's face and her good mood started to dissipate. The expression certainly suggested that Davidia's snake hadn't slithered back into its basket in the night. Not that Liz had expected it would, but she could always hope.

Then Liz's gaze met Harriet's, and the petite woman's face brightened. Liz almost groaned aloud. Another lengthy dream premonition would definitely kill the rest of her good mood. Suddenly, she had an idea. "Can I have everyone's attention for a moment?"

Everybody turned to her, even Brya, who sat up straight so quickly that Liz was mildly suspicious the little girl had been doing something Liz wouldn't appreciate.

Clinging to the fraying shreds of her morning optimism, Liz fished the green crystal out of her pocket and held it out. "I seem to have picked this up somewhere, maybe yesterday. It's such a pretty little thing, and I wonder if it fell from someone's jewelry or perhaps an adornment on a purse or clothing."

Davidia moved closer to examine the stone. "I don't have anything with sparkly bits, but that is certainly a pretty shade of green."

Brya scrambled up on her knees in the chair and leaned across the table. "Can I have it?"

"Sweetheart," Courtney said, "don't climb on the table."

Brya ignored her mother, her whole attention on Liz. "Can I? Please?"

Liz gave her a pointed look but didn't speak.

With a sigh, Brya scooted back into her chair properly. "Now can I have it?"

"I need to see if I can find the owner," Liz said. "But if the owner doesn't turn up, I don't see why not."

Brya frowned. "How long do I have to wait?"

"Until I'm done searching for the owner," Liz responded.

"Everyone is here," the little girl said. "No one owns it. You should give it to me."

"Now, Brya," her mother said. "If you're going to be cranky, Liz could decide to keep it."

"No, she couldn't," Brya said. "She already said I could have it. She can't change her mind now. That would be lying."

Sorry that she'd ever mentioned anything, Liz gave the child a stern look. "I will return the crystal to the owner if I can find her, but if not, I will let you have it."

Brya flung herself against the back of her chair, making it scoot slightly. She crossed her arms over her chest and glared at all of them.

The other guests at the table simply ignored the sullen child and continued with their breakfast. As Brya had pointed out, no one claimed the little green crystal, so Liz dropped it back into her shirt pocket. She may have made the child a promise, but she imagined having to wait a little while would be good for her.

When breakfast was over, Sarah entered and began collecting the plates to carry to the kitchen.

Liz smiled at her and would have joined her in clearing the table, but Davidia caught her arm and whispered, "Have you made any headway on finding Cleopatra?"

"Not yet," Liz admitted, "but I haven't given up. I want Cleopatra locked up in her basket as much as you do. I'm hoping no one finds her in their bed."

Davidia harrumphed. "That's not going to happen. I tell you, she didn't escape. She was taken. You need to search everyone's room."

"I won't be doing that," Liz said. "But when we clean each room today, we will keep an eye out. If someone has your pet, I'm sure we'll find her."

"I hope so. You're lucky it's not too cold in here. If my poor darling comes down with a cold because you rented a room to a snake thief, I will hold you responsible."

Liz winced at the word *snake* and glanced around, but the rest of the guests had already exited the room. "Please don't worry. We will find her soon."

Davidia seemed anything but convinced, but she left the room.

Liz picked up the coffee mugs to return to the kitchen. As she circled the table, she spotted Beans lurking underneath it near Brya's chair. The dog wasn't allowed in the dining room during meals or really anytime. "You know you're not supposed to be in here."

Beans looked up at her and burped in reply.

Liz set the coffee mugs back on the table and knelt to inspect Beans. She noticed bits of eggs and herbs in his whiskers. Clearly, Brya had been sneaking him food. She hefted the chubby dog in her arms and carried him out to his favorite rug, assuming he'd want a nap after stuffing himself on frittata.

Grabbing the mugs as she headed back through the dining room, Liz pondered exactly where the snake could have hidden. Though she'd only seen it coiled up, she expected the creature was at least four feet long, so it would need a fairly large hiding spot. She thought they'd searched everywhere. Where could it be?

When she reached the kitchen, she found Sarah washing the dishes, her arms deep in soapy water. Though the inn had a fine dishwasher, the Amish girl always washed the dishes by hand unless Liz got to them first.

"You don't have to do the dishes, you know," she said.

"Yes, ma'am, I know," Sarah said quietly. "But it is too early to get into the guest rooms to clean, and I don't like to be idle."

"I cannot even imagine you being idle," Liz said. "By the way, how is Isaac doing? I haven't seen him lately." Sarah had been single when Liz first hired her, but she married Isaac soon after. At first Liz had worried that married life would take away the most fantastic helper Liz had ever had, but Sarah continued working part-time.

"He is well. *Dänka*."

"I'm glad to hear it." Liz retrieved a clean dish towel from the drawer and started drying the dishes that Sarah had washed. "Remember to keep an eye out for the snake as you clean this morning."

Sarah nodded.

"Oh, there is something else." Liz took the crystal from her pocket and held it out to show Sarah. "I ended up with this in my tote bag yesterday, but I don't know where I picked it up. I don't use the bag often, so it could have been in there for months. Does it look familiar to you?"

Sarah studied the little stone without touching it. "It is very pretty. I have never seen anything like it up close. The community does not own such things."

"I'm sure it isn't real," Liz said. "I thought it might have come off an article of clothing or jewelry belonging to one of our guests."

"Perhaps it came from the quilt shop," Sarah said. "I know there are many embellishments for sale there. Sometimes I like to look at them, though I would never use them in my sewing."

"That's an excellent idea." She glanced around the kitchen. "If you feel like you can handle the rest of the cleanup, I'll go and ask Mary Ann and Sadie about it."

"It is little work," Sarah said. "I can do it."

"You are the real gem around here," Liz told her as she headed across the kitchen for the door. She wasn't sure why she wanted to find the owner of the little crystal so much. Maybe because she seemed to be piling up strange incidents with the death of Nora at the courthouse and then the missing snake. Finding one answer, even to such a trivial question, would make her feel better.

The quilt shop was bustling. Liz spotted Harriet picking through bundles of charm packs that featured small pieces of fabric in colors and patterns that went well together. She also spotted a number of women who looked vaguely familiar. They weren't inn guests, but she'd seen them often at the quilt shop. Sometimes it was easy to forget that the quilt shop wasn't just an extension of the inn. It was a busy store drawing people from all over Pleasant Creek and beyond.

As Liz waited for a chance to approach the counter without getting in the way of customers, she recognized some familiar faces, an Amish woman and two little girls, who walked in from the sunny workroom. Liz's face lit up at the sight of her dear friend and cousin Miriam Borkholder with her two young daughters Grace and Keturah.

Miriam was walking while rooting through a plain basket and didn't see Liz, but the two girls noticed her and their faces brightened with sweet smiles. Keturah tugged at her mother's arm and whispered something to her that caused Miriam to look up with a warm welcome.

"Liz, I was hoping to see you." Miriam held out her hand, and Liz took it.

The two little girls stood silently beside their mother, and Liz was struck by the difference between their attentive attitudes and Brya's grumpiness during breakfast.

"I was asking Sarah about Isaac a little while ago," Liz said. Miriam was Isaac's mother. Like many of the Amish, she had a big family, but she never seemed frazzled by meeting the needs of so many.

"I am certain Sarah told you Isaac is well," Miriam said. "Though he is busy, as are we all. Summer always rushes by with many things to do."

"I've always found that to be the case," Liz agreed. "The inn had a busy fall and winter too. Quilting seems to pair well with chilly weather and cozy fireplaces."

"This is true. I do much of my quilting in the winter." Miriam smiled at her daughters. "But today I am buying fabrics for a new dress for Keturah, who is growing like summer grain."

Keturah stood up very straight beside her older sister, as if to emphasize her recently increased height. She wouldn't boast about it, as that was not the Amish way, but it didn't mean she didn't enjoy hearing it mentioned.

"I noticed she seemed taller," Liz said, giving the little girl a smile. "And Grace is nearly as tall as you."

Miriam nodded, then said, "I hope you will come out to visit with us soon. I know the *Kinder* would love to have you as much as I."

"I can show you the new foal," Keturah said. "She has such long legs."

"I would like that." A trip out to the Borkholders' farm sounded absolutely wonderful to Liz. It really would be like a little vacation and much more relaxing than her unfortunate morning of jury duty.

As the Amish weren't ones for idle chatter, Miriam soon excused herself to pay for her purchases. A few minutes later she herded her daughters out of the shop, leaving a rare moment of quiet at the front counter.

Sadie raised her eyebrows as Liz rushed over. "What's on the agenda today, snakes or murder?"

Liz looked around in alarm, but the two ladies perusing a rack of brightly colored thread spools didn't seem to have been startled by Sadie's odd question. "Neither. I have something I wanted to show you." She held out the green crystal. "Sarah mentioned that this might be one of the embellishments you sell here. I seem to have picked it up somewhere. Honestly, I don't remember where I got it, but I discovered it in my tote bag last night when I was cleaning it out."

Mary Ann leaned closer to Liz's hand. "It looks like a real gemstone. It's certainly a real crystal, not acrylic like the ones we carry. The shop doesn't have any embellishments that look so authentic. Maybe you picked it up at the courthouse."

"I don't know. I can't believe I don't remember where I found it."

"May I see it?" Sadie asked. Liz handed it over, and Sadie held it up to the light. "I agree with Mary Ann; this looks real."

"I'm sure it's not. An emerald that size would be worth a fortune," Liz said. "I would know because I have a pair of earrings that have real emeralds, teeny tiny ones. I can't even imagine what a jewel this size would be worth."

"Maybe you should take it to a jeweler and find out," Sadie suggested.

Liz didn't think she'd enjoy being laughed at for carrying a pretty piece of green-faceted glass into a jeweler, which was what she believed she had. "I think I'll hold off on having it appraised," she said as she slid the stone into her pocket.

"Did anyone find the lost pet last night?" Mary Ann asked. "I have to admit, the thought of it is making me nervous."

"Yeah," Sadie said loudly, causing Liz to cringe. She pointed at a pile of long, thin "draft dodgers" at the end of the counter. "This morning one of those fell off the counter, and I was sure it was the snake. I nearly jumped a foot off the floor."

"Snake?" One of the women from the thread rack had wandered closer to the counter. "You don't get snakes inside buildings here, do you?"

"No," Liz said. "We've never had any wild snakes wander into the inn."

"I should hope not," the woman said. "I hate snakes."

"Snakes are actually very helpful creatures," Mary Ann said, always one to look on the bright side. "They eat mice, for one thing, and mice are destructive pests for farmers around here."

The woman shuddered. "The farmers can have them." She quickly paid for her thread and hurried out, glancing around nervously as she went.

"See," Liz said. "That's exactly the kind of thing I'm worried about."

"Yes, it would be bad if folks knew there was a snake loose in the inn," Sadie boomed.

"A snake!"

Liz turned, her stomach sinking into her shoes as she spotted Harriet standing inside the doorway to the shop.

"What do you mean, there's a snake loose in the inn?" Harriet squealed.

"It's nothing to worry about," Liz said gently. "There are no dangerous animals in the inn."

Harriet narrowed her eyes. "I should have known. I dreamed about yarn all night."

"Yarn?" Mary Ann echoed from behind Liz. "How does yarn relate to snakes?"

"It's long and thin like a snake," Harriet said, her tone suggesting the answer was incredibly obvious. "Symbols. Dreams are all about symbols."

Liz took a deep breath. "Well, this particular creature is about as dangerous as yarn. One of our guests has lost her pet, but we're looking for it, and it will soon be back where it belongs."

Harriet stared at Liz goggle-eyed. "You let someone check in with a snake?"

Liz stammered for a moment while she tried to come up with a good answer.

"I'll do something in town while you conduct this search for the snake," Harriet continued. "But if you haven't found it when I get back, I will go someplace else to spend the night. I have enough trouble sleeping as it is." The little woman spun on her heel and marched out of the shop.

Liz watched her go, certain that if the snake wasn't located soon, there would be more guests doing exactly the same thing.

7

The arrival of a new guest drew Liz's attention away from fretting about the potential exodus of her other guests. With the strange events of the last twenty-four hours, Liz had nearly forgotten she had another reservation.

Gwen Paulson was tall, made taller still by her ramrod straight posture that reminded Liz of her godson, Steve, and she wondered if her new guest had also spent time in the military. The woman carried a tapestry-covered bag and eyed Beans with obvious disapproval.

Beans showed no sign of being bothered by Gwen's displeasure and slept through the whole check-in process.

"I'm always amazed by people thinking animals belong in the house," Gwen huffed.

Surprised, Liz said, "Our pet-friendly policy is on our website."

Gwen gave Liz a look only slightly warmer than the one she'd offered Beans. "I didn't say it wasn't your right to bring animals into your home, only that it surprises me. It's a desire I don't share."

"You aren't allergic, are you?" Liz asked as the horrifying image of Nora during her allergic reaction flashed through her mind.

"No, my distaste is aesthetic, not health related." Gwen glanced around the room with interest. "I booked this inn because of its connection with quilting, which is my passion. I can abide a single slobbery dog as long as he doesn't come into my room."

How nice of you, Liz thought wryly. "Beans never leaves the first floor. May I show you up? You're in the Amish Room. I think you'll find it cozy and comfortable."

Gwen responded with a single nod. "I approve of the Amish very much. They're an efficient people."

Liz supposed that was true, though it wasn't the first thing that came to her mind when she thought of her Amish friends. She led the new guest upstairs, and as they reached the second-floor landing, Brya burst out of the Rose of Sharon Room, plowing right into Gwen. The child bounced off the tall woman and stumbled backward.

Gwen caught Brya by the arm to keep her from falling. "Stair landings are no place for running," she said sharply.

Brya scowled at her. "Let go."

Gwen released the child's arm.

Brya took a step back, still scowling. "I'm a guest too. I can do what I want!"

"Actually, you can't." Courtney marched out of the room and took Brya by the hand, then turned to Liz and Gwen. "I'm sorry. Sometimes Brya gets overexcited."

Gwen gazed down her nose at the slightly shorter woman. "Perhaps she's bored. A quilting-themed bed-and-breakfast hardly seems like a stimulating place for a child."

"She's learning to quilt," Courtney said. "She loves it."

Brya's rolling eyes made Liz doubt it.

"Your room is right over there," Liz told Gwen and gestured farther down the hall, hoping to separate the two women before real conflict erupted.

When they entered the Amish Room, Gwen scrutinized it with obvious approval. The huge walnut bed, with its simple lines, had a bench-like love seat attached to its footboard. A quilt appliquéd with silhouettes of Amish figures and scenes against blue, gold, and dark red backgrounds covered the bed. Gwen walked over and placed her bag on the love seat. "This will do me very well."

"I'm so glad." Liz told her briefly about the coffee hour later in the afternoon and handed her a brochure with some events going on in the Pleasant Creek area in the next few days.

"Thank you," Gwen said. "Though I don't intend to be frolicking around the countryside. I'm here to quilt."

"Then I do hope you enjoy it." Liz left Gwen to settle in and headed down to the kitchen to bake the cookies for the social hour she'd mentioned. She often used frozen gourmet cookie dough for her afternoon treats, but today she decided to try something a bit more adventurous and bake lemon bars. The brightness of lemon always made her think of summer.

After Liz prepared the bottom crust for the bars and popped it into the oven to prebake, she sliced into the lemons. The scent that filled the kitchen seemed to wrap around her like a hug, and it lifted her spirits. This was why she loved being an innkeeper. Peaceful moments like this had occurred far too rarely when she was a high-powered corporate patent attorney in Boston.

Soon Liz found herself humming under her breath as she squeezed the lemons and beat the juice into sugar and eggs and flour for the upper half of the bars. She poured the lemony filling over the baked crust and slid the pan back into the oven.

The lemon bars had just hit the cooling rack when Liz's bliss was interrupted by the ringing of her phone. She pulled it out of her pocket and felt her joy pop like a soap bubble. The call was from the police chief. *Don't panic. Maybe it's something good.* No part of her believed it, but she tried to stay positive as she pushed the button to connect the call.

"The coroner found a bee tangled in Ms. Wexler's hair," the chief said with none of his usual folksy preamble. "And another caught up in her clothes."

"So it was an accident," Liz said, feeling oddly relieved. She had come into contact with far too much murder and mayhem since moving to Pleasant Creek. "She must have walked through the garden after all."

"Maybe not. Both bees were coated with an odd residue, so I had it tested. It turns out to be a prescription medication for depression.

Now, either our busy little bees were depressed, or they spent some time in someone's pill bottle. And that suggests foul play to me."

"Perhaps Nora brought them with her. It could have been suicide," Liz suggested. Then she thought of the woman's swollen face and the way she had struggled to breathe. Liz couldn't imagine that Nora—or anyone else—would choose to kill herself in such a manner.

"I'm not ruling it out," Chief Houghton said, "but I'm doubtful. I would like to come by later in the day or sometime tomorrow to ask you a few more questions."

"Surely you're not still considering the silly notion that I had a violent encounter with her," Liz said. "Nora was a perfect stranger. I would never go through some elaborate plan to kill her."

"Of course not," he said agreeably. "But I'd still like to chat with you. You were a witness and one of the few people with Ms. Wexler after she was stung and before she lost consciousness."

"Fine. You can come over anytime. I should be here for the rest of the day, and I don't have plans for tomorrow either."

Chief Houghton thanked her, and they ended the call with him projecting what she was sure was a false cheerfulness. Despite that, she was completely grumpy. She felt terrible for the dead woman, no matter how obnoxious she'd been. But she also wondered how she'd somehow managed to get herself entangled in another investigation. Why did things like this keep happening to her?

Liz began cleaning up the kitchen, scrubbing the counter with a vengeance to work off some of her annoyance. While she scrubbed, she thought about what she knew about Nora Wexler. The woman had been part of the Amish community at one time. Liz wondered idly if Miriam might have known her. The community was quite close, so it seemed likely, though with Nora's offensive comments about the Amish, Liz doubted Miriam would welcome a conversation about her. Liz definitely didn't want to alienate her dear friend.

When the kitchen was back to its usual immaculate cleanliness, Liz picked up the pan of lemon bars, wondering if they'd cooled enough to cut. She had forgotten to set a timer because of the chief's phone call. As she held the pan close to her face to breathe in the smell, a bloodcurdling scream sounded from upstairs.

8

Liz nearly dropped the pan of lemon bars.

Another scream followed. It sounded like someone was being murdered.

After a dash up the curving stairs, Liz spotted several guests milling around the second-floor landing, appearing bewildered and afraid. She assumed someone in the group had reacted to finding the missing snake, so she directed her attention to the floor and the bottom of the walls. Nothing long and green slithered anywhere in sight.

"Did any of you scream?" Liz asked.

They shook their heads.

After a quick head count, Liz realized that Gwen was not on the landing. Liz heard another scream that came from the Amish Room and hurried over to the oak door. "Mrs. Paulson," she called, "are you all right?"

Only a shriek replied.

Liz tried the doorknob and found the door unlocked. "I'm coming in."

Gwen stood on the love seat that connected to the big walnut bed. The tall woman's head nearly brushed the ceiling, and she shifted slightly as if she wished she could get farther away from the floor. Her eyes were open so wide that white showed almost completely around her brown irises. She gestured with a shaking hand toward the highboy across the room. One drawer of the dresser was partly open, making it the only thing out of place in the entire room.

Liz approached the dresser with caution. She had a pretty good idea what lurked in the drawer, but that didn't mean she wasn't leery. Finally, she reached the point where she could peek over the edge of the drawer. Nestled inside amidst neatly folded clothes was the same bright green snake she'd been searching for so diligently.

Liz turned around slowly.

Gwen had stopped shrieking, but she had backed away so that she was crouched on the quilt at the foot of the bed.

"It's okay," Liz said calmly. "That snake isn't poisonous."

Gwen spoke through clenched teeth. "Then get it out of here."

"Hold on." Liz stepped into the hall where she spotted Davidia not far from the doorway. She motioned to the woman. "Could you come inside, please?"

Davidia's face brightened, and she sprinted through the doorway. "Where is she?"

Liz pointed at the dresser.

Davidia rushed over to the highboy and carefully lifted the snake out, cooing to it the whole time.

"That creature was in the inn on purpose?" Gwen demanded, finally lowering herself to sit cross-legged on the bed but still not climbing down.

"Cleopatra is my quilting muse," Davidia said.

"How did the snake get inside the drawer?" Liz asked.

Davidia and Gwen spoke in unison. "That's what *I'd* like to know."

Liz turned to Gwen. "Did you leave the drawer open, even a crack?"

"Of course not," Gwen snapped. "I am not in the habit of sloppy housekeeping, even when on vacation. I came upstairs from doing some shopping at Sew Welcome, and I decided to change my blouse as I was feeling rather warm. I pulled out the drawer and saw the snake."

"And scared poor Cleopatra half to death with all that screaming, I'm sure," Davidia said, cuddling the snake in her arms.

Liz bent to examine the way the drawer fit into the highboy. "With the drawer completely closed, I don't know how the snake got into the drawer."

"Clearly, either the drawer was left open . . . ," Davidia said.

"Which it wasn't," Gwen insisted.

". . . or someone put Cleopatra into the drawer on purpose," Davidia continued as if Gwen hadn't spoken. She glared at Liz. "I told you someone stole my snake, and you didn't believe me."

"I never said I didn't believe you," Liz replied.

"You didn't have to say it." Davidia sniffed. "I could tell."

"Thankfully, you have the snake back now," Liz said. "And I do hope Cleopatra stays contained for the rest of your stay."

"That creature is going to continue to stay in the inn?" Gwen asked.

"I will keep her hamper locked," Davidia said. "As well as my room door. I had Cleo's hamper latched, but I admit to leaving my door unlocked when I wasn't in the room. I didn't think this was the kind of inn where one had to lock one's door to avoid stealing."

"Stealing has never been a problem here before," Liz said, "but keeping your room locked when you're not in it is wise, no matter where you are."

Davidia left the room, cuddling the snake and speaking quietly to it.

Liz followed closely behind, wanting to see the reactions of the people on the landing when Davidia walked out. For the most part, everyone looked equally shocked and alarmed at the sight of a long, green snake woven through the hands of an inn guest. Only one person looked unsurprised and amused.

Then Liz remembered the sharp words Gwen had directed at Brya when the two connected on the landing when Gwen had arrived. She couldn't believe she hadn't suspected the mischievous little girl when the snake first disappeared. *I blame distraction over the murder.*

Before taking on the little girl and her mother, Liz returned to Gwen's room. Gwen had finally climbed down from the bed and stood near the door with her usual ramrod straight posture.

"I will be happy to refund your money for your stay and find you another room in Pleasant Creek," Liz said. "I'm so sorry you had to go through this ordeal."

Gwen smiled slightly. "Actually, I found the whole experience interesting. It's been a few years since I have faced anything that was quite so invigorating. I would prefer not to encounter the snake again, but I don't intend to leave the inn."

Liz felt a rush of relief that nearly made her dizzy. Now if only the rest of the guests would feel the same way. But first, she intended to deal with the issue of dangerous pranks. "I'm very grateful for your understanding. If you'll excuse me, I think I have an idea about how the snake got into your dresser, and I need to deal with it."

Liz had barely gone a step when Gwen called out to her, "Could I possibly use your washing machine? I know it isn't part of the normal guest facilities, but I would rather not wear anything in that dresser drawer until it is laundered."

"Of course," Liz said. She gave Gwen directions to the utility room downstairs where the washer and dryer were located.

Some of the guests still lingered on the landing. They had apparently recovered from the shock of seeing a snake inside the bed-and-breakfast because as soon as they noticed Liz they barraged her with questions.

Liz held up her hands. "The snake belongs to a guest. It will be very carefully locked up from this moment forward. There are no other pets in the inn at this time except for Beans, whom most of you have already met."

A few people grumbled, but only the young couple who'd been staying in the Heirloom Room announced that they would be checking out immediately. Since they were due to leave the next day anyway, the loss of revenue was far less than Liz had feared.

"It's perfectly understandable," she said soothingly to them. "I'm sorry for the upset."

"You should be," the wife snapped before whirling around and marching to her room.

The husband gave Liz an apologetic smile. "It's been great, but Jenny is terrified of snakes."

"I can understand that," Liz replied. "I'll be downstairs by the time you're packed."

"Thank you." He turned and followed his wife to the room.

Most of the rest of the guests had returned to their rooms. Liz spotted Courtney attempting to herd Brya back to their room, but the little girl seemed reluctant to go.

Liz crossed the landing and bent to look the child in the eye. "You shouldn't have taken Miss Burke's snake. She was very worried."

"My daughter didn't take anyone's belongings," Courtney said, but Liz could tell her heart wasn't in the denial, not with Brya's face reflecting her guilt so unmistakenly.

Straightening back up, Liz said, "Yes, she did. I don't know why she took the snake, but I know why she put it in Mrs. Paulson's room." She looked into Brya's face again. "You were angry because she snapped at you."

Brya crossed her arms over her chest defiantly. "I was playing. She shouldn't have yelled at me."

Courtney stared at her daughter in wide-eyed alarm. "Did you take the snake?"

Brya shrugged. "It was pretty. I was just going to play with it for a little while. You never let me have a pet."

"Because your father is allergic to fur," her mother said. "We've talked about this before."

"Snakes don't have fur. Can I have a snake?" Brya begged.

"I'll have to think about that for a long time." Courtney turned to Liz. "I'm so sorry for all the trouble. Sometimes Brya can be a handful."

"Clearly."

Brya stepped closer to Liz and tugged on the hem of her

blouse. "Are you done looking for the owner of the green crystal? Can I have it?"

Liz shook her head. "I'm still looking for the owner." *And I'm certainly not going to reward you for your behavior*, she added in her head.

Brya frowned, and Liz felt a twinge of worry, wondering what else the little prankster might do.

9

After Brya stomped off behind her mother, Liz turned to discover Gwen standing in her doorway, watching the little girl with a thoughtful expression. Liz offered the woman a smile, but Gwen merely backed into her room and closed the door.

Well, at least the snake is back in the basket, Liz thought, trying to count her blessings where she could.

In the foyer downstairs, Liz found a surprise. There was a young woman holding a small tartan-printed pet carrier and a matching suitcase. The woman's black curls bounced slightly as she rocked on her toes, obviously waiting. Nearby, Beans zeroed in on the pet carrier, his stumpy tail wagging. The woman ignored him, and she even stepped to one side when Beans crept closer to sniff the carrier.

Liz found something about the woman vaguely familiar, though she was fairly certain they'd never met. She was still trying to figure out what was triggering that nagging sense of familiarity as she said, "May I help you?"

"I'd like to check in," the woman said. "I don't have a reservation, but I was hoping you had a room. I live here in Pleasant Creek, well, actually right outside of town, but my house is being painted. My dog, Pixie, is sensitive to the fumes, so I thought we might spend a few days here while the house airs out."

That explained the familiarity. Liz had probably seen the woman in the grocery store or somewhere else in town. Pleasant Creek was small enough that it seemed likely they'd crossed paths before. With one mystery solved, she did some quick calculations in her head. The Heirloom Room was about to become empty, but she needed time to clean it, and she hated to leave the woman downstairs to wait, even if she didn't have a reservation. Plus, she wasn't sure the little dog and the snake should both be housed on the same floor. It was possible that the smell of the snake could make the dog bark and annoy the other guests.

"I'm pretty full," Liz said, "but I do have the Sunset Room on the third floor available. It shares a bath with the other third-floor room, but no one is staying in there right now. You'd have the floor to yourself."

"That sounds perfect." The woman lifted the pet carrier close to her face and said in a squeaky voice, "Isn't it, sweetie?"

If the dog had an opinion, she kept it to herself. Liz was pleased that she seemed to be a quiet dog, having reacted neither to Beans nor to her owner squeaking in her face. With the week Liz was having, she really didn't need any more disruptions.

As she checked in the young woman, she learned that her name was Jessica Ellis. Thankfully, Sarah kept all the rooms made up immaculately, and the Sunset Room was no exception, so Liz was able to lead the woman and her dog upstairs immediately.

When they reached the Sunset Room, Jessica set the pet carrier down on the floor and walked over to the windows, pushing aside one of the delicate lace curtains. "Oh, what a lovely view. Is that Jaynes Lake?"

"It is. And you can see the sunset over the lake from here, which is why we call this the Sunset Room." Liz went on to tell her about the coffee hour later in the day, then held out her hands. "Normally, this is where I give out a brochure of scheduled upcoming local activities, but I don't imagine you need it. I can get you one, though, if you're interested."

Jessica smiled, and a dimple appeared in her cheek. "Thanks, but I'm looking forward to a couple of quiet days relaxing. If I have to be run out of my house, I'm going to turn it into a short vacation."

That viewpoint reminded Liz of Naomi's words about jury duty. For her new guest's sake, Liz hoped her vacation worked out better than the one Liz had recently experienced.

As Liz walked back downstairs, she noted that the second floor seemed quiet, and no one waited with requests for her on the first floor either. She wondered if she could sneak into her quarters and put her feet up for a few minutes. She made it as far as the kitchen when she heard knocking on the outside door of the utility room. With a groan, she remembered that Chief Houghton was dropping by for more questions.

Sure enough, she spotted the chief as soon as she entered the room. She recognized his usual harmless, slightly rumpled look that tended to lull people into blurting out hidden truths. Thankfully, Liz had no hidden truths to blurt out.

She led Chief Houghton to the kitchen, poured him a cup of coffee, and gave him a lemon square, though she told herself that she was only being hospitable, not trying to soften him up. After all, she hadn't done anything wrong. Liz had no idea where all the guilt was coming from. Maybe she felt bad about not saving Nora, which was silly. She wasn't a doctor, and she'd done what she could.

Chief Houghton dabbed at the corners of his mouth with the napkin she handed him. "Right now, the only person anyone remembers having issues with Ms. Wexler is you, but it's been my experience that you're considerably more perceptive than the average person." He pulled out his notebook from his pocket and flipped it open. "So, what did you see?"

"I saw an angry woman who seemed to have an ax to grind with everyone," Liz replied. "She said some very offensive things about the Amish community. I know I'm not the only one who didn't enjoy them. In fact, I remember noticing one woman's face in particular who seemed to be reacting very strongly. She looked like she hated Nora Wexler."

"Fortunately, looks cannot actually kill," the chief said. "Still, give me a description of the woman, and I'll check her out."

Liz thought about it. "She was probably a few years younger than me. Her hair was dark, and she wore it in a long bob like Mary Ann's.

She was nicely dressed, but I can't recall what she wore exactly, just that I had that impression of her. She may have been pretty, but with so much anger on her face, it was hard to tell."

Chief Houghton huffed as he jotted down notes. "I'll see if the jury clerk can match a name to that description. She hasn't been a fountain of help, as she doesn't seem particularly observant."

"I noticed that she seemed distracted," Liz agreed.

He shrugged. "She was probably bored. Can you imagine doing that job day after day? Check people in, keep them corralled, and let them go. It sounds like day care without the bottles and diapers."

"At least the clerk didn't have any negative exchanges with Nora. She wasn't even in the room when Nora was bad-mouthing the Amish." Then Liz had a thought. "Nora also went on and on about her ex-husband. She said he was trying to cheat her out of something that was hers. She didn't give any specifics, though, but she was certainly angry at him and his lawyer."

Chief Houghton took a sip of his coffee, then gestured with the little bit of lemon square he had left. "Exes are great suspects. I'll look into him and see what he was doing on Tuesday." He harrumphed. "I'm slowly going from no suspects to far too many."

"Well, you can cross me off the suspect list," Liz said brightly. "That should lighten the load."

He smiled but didn't respond.

Liz felt a pinch of alarm. Did the police chief really consider her a potential murderer? She thought about asking him, but she couldn't quite get up the nerve in case the answer wasn't the one she wanted.

Chief Houghton popped the last of the lemon square into his mouth and chased it with the rest of the coffee. "Thanks for the treat, but I need to get going. I'm driving out to talk to Ms. Wexler's neighbors. It's been my experience that neighbors can be a good source of information about who's mad at whom."

"Does she live out near the Amish community?" Liz asked. "She mentioned that she'd grown up in it."

The chief raised his eyebrows. "She seems like an unlikely member of the Amish community."

"It's what she said during jury duty."

"Actually, she lives near the high school. It's the big, gray Victorian that's all chopped up to make apartments." He smiled wryly. "Apparently, Ms. Wexler is responsible for that questionable remodel, so maybe one of her neighbors killed her for lowering the property values."

"That seems a stretch," Liz said.

"I've seen more unlikely motives."

"Now that I think of it, I know the house you're talking about." Liz had been to the high school for basketball games, and since she loved looking at houses, she'd noticed the ones she passed on the way to the school. It would have been hard to miss that particular Victorian because it was so hideous. "The outside stairs to the second floor is one of the ugliest additions I've ever seen. And that house must have been beautiful when it was young."

Chief Houghton chuckled as he slipped his notebook back into his pocket. "A lot of old things and people were." He thanked Liz for her help, and she walked him to the door.

After he left, Liz contemplated the idea of driving over to Nora's house later and poking around. If the chief was still considering her a suspect, it might be worthwhile to help look for the real killer. Of course, that kind of thinking had gotten her into trouble before.

I'll ask Mary Ann and Sadie for their advice, Liz decided and headed to Sew Welcome. She found Mary Ann alone in the shop. Since she knew Sadie wasn't in the kitchen searching for a snack, Liz wondered aloud at her absence.

"It's your fault," Mary Ann said with a light laugh. "The whole downstairs smells like lemon bars. Sadie said she had to choose between raiding the coffee hour snack or making a run to Sweet Everything."

"I'm sure Naomi will appreciate her decision." Liz gestured to several cut lengths of cloth on the counter. "What are you doing with those?"

"Miriam wanted some very specific fabric that she'd bought in the past, but I was out," Mary Ann explained as she wrapped the cloth in plain craft paper. "I told her it would be a few days before another shipment came in. Then the delivery arrived early, so I thought I would drop off her order after the shop closes today. That way she won't have to make another trip into town."

With the chief's visit so fresh in her mind, Liz realized that she should have asked Miriam about Nora Wexler. She was often hesitant to risk offending her cousin, but even though she'd made a few blunders along the way, the two only seemed to grow closer. "I could drive out with the fabrics," Liz offered. "I can be back before the coffee hour, and I'm not expecting any new guests."

Mary Ann handed over the wrapped package. "That would be terrific. I need to stop at the grocery store on my way home, but I was going to put it off to deliver this."

The drive out to the Borkholder farm was beautiful with bright sun and lush green fields on either side of the road. Liz made good time, only once slowed by an Amish buggy pulled by a dappled-gray horse.

Miriam was waiting on the front porch of the white farmhouse by the time Liz had shut off the car. She walked out to meet Liz, her serene smile as welcoming as if it had been weeks since she'd last seen Liz instead of just hours.

"You must be eager to see the foal," Miriam said. "Keturah will be so pleased when she and her sister come back from the neighbor's farm. I hope you can wait for them."

"I will be glad to visit the barn with Keturah, but I really came on an errand for Mary Ann." She held up the package. "Your cloth arrived early."

Miriam clapped once softly. "Very good. I was hoping to start on the dresses right away." She gestured toward the porch. "Please come in."

"As long as I'm not interrupting anything." Liz fell in step beside Miriam as they walked toward the house. "I actually do have a question I'd like to ask you."

"Oh?"

"It's about someone I met when I went to the courthouse for jury duty. The woman said she'd been raised in the Amish community," Liz said. "Nora Wexler."

Miriam stopped abruptly and looked at Liz with large, solemn eyes. "Ja, Nora grew up here, and I knew her. But her name was not Wexler then. It was Brauner."

"If it's not too upsetting, I'd like to know about her."

Miriam sighed. "Come and share a cup of tea with me. I will tell you a sad story."

Following Miriam into the house, Liz was struck, as always, by how lovely and homey it was. Before moving to Pleasant Creek, Liz had expected the Amish to live in cramped, plain, and dark homes, but Miriam's kitchen was bright and welcoming. An old metal pitcher on the table was full of cut flowers from Miriam's garden. The sweet scent of the flowers mixed with a delicious smell coming from a cooling rack filled with cookies.

"I am making *Kekse* from a recipe I learned from your aunt Ruth," Miriam said. "You should have one. If you like them, I can copy out the recipe for you."

"I'd like that," Liz said. She was constantly collecting bits and pieces from her mother's past since she'd moved to Pleasant Creek in search of information about her family. Miriam had been a huge help in that search, and Liz had come to love her like a sister.

Soon settled with a cup of hot tea and a molasses cookie, Liz waited patiently for Miriam to return to the topic of Nora Wexler. She took a bite of the warm, soft cookie, and her mouth filled with the flavors of spice and sugar. She definitely needed this recipe. Her guests at the inn would love the delicious treat.

Miriam smiled at Liz's obvious pleasure, then took a long sip of her tea. After setting the cup down, she said, "When we were children, I knew Nora Brauner very well, though we were not the same age." She smiled slightly. "Children of different ages mix and play together much more in the community than amongst the English, or so I am told. Even as a young child, Nora always had an unseemly temper, and she was often in trouble with the elders."

"I witnessed her temper when I met her," Liz said.

"It was hard to miss, but her temper wasn't all of her. She also had a sadness, and I often tried to cheer her. When she was quite young, Nora was stung by a bee in the schoolhouse garden where we were pulling weeds. She nearly died. Her mother was terrified of losing her after that, and I believe it played a large part in Nora's sadness and her anger."

"How is that?"

"As you know, we in the community often have large families, but Nora's mother wasn't able to have any more children. So Nora was doubly special to her. Her mother kept Nora extremely close. The child chafed under all the restrictions. Her mother barely let her go outside, and Nora spent most of her time in the family's tiny shop. She would sneak away, but that only made her mother hold her more tightly."

"It sounds lonely," Liz said, her cookie and tea forgotten as she listened to the unhappy tale.

Miriam ran her finger around the rim of her cup. "I think she was lonely. As we aged, more and more of Nora's friends turned away from her wildness and her anger. Only one stayed close. Prudence Spratt."

Liz brightened. "Oh, maybe I could talk to her."

"Prudence is no longer in the community either. I could not tell you how to find her. When Nora was old enough for her Rumschpringe, she ran far from home and took Prudence with her. I believe it was always Prudence's nature to follow, and Nora was a strong leader."

"It sounds like I need to find Prudence," Liz said. "If they're close friends, she'd know who might want to hurt Nora."

Miriam shook her head. "I do not think Prudence and Nora were close for long after they left. Nora had fallen in love with an English man she met in her mother's shop. It is for him that she left the community, but she took Prudence along so she would not be alone if the romance did not work. I believe Nora married the man."

"If she did, it didn't last," Liz said. "She expressed anger and resentment toward her ex-husband."

Miriam took another sip of tea. "Prudence tried to return to the community. Nora had abandoned her after her marriage to the English man, and she realized her friend had only taken her along as a kind of backup plan. Of course, Prudence was welcome to rejoin us, but she could never quite adapt to our ways again. I could see she was lost because she felt neither Amish nor English. We tried to help, but she left. I do not know where she is."

"That is a sad story," Liz said.

"Yes, when I think of Nora and Prudence, I picture them when we were girls with long braids, but the years change us all. I have received so much blessing from Gött, but Prudence is lost in the world and Nora has died." Her voice thickened as she spoke, and though Miriam didn't give in to tears, her eyes shone as she grieved for her friends.

10

Miriam's young daughters came home a little while later, and Liz was treated to a visit with the new foal. The wobbly legged creature was beautiful with a chestnut coat and a patch of white on her nose like a star.

"She likes to be petted," Keturah said. "And I know she'll like apples, but *Vater* says she cannot have them until she is older."

"I'm sure that's right," Liz said. "Your father knows a great deal about horses."

"Vater knows *all* about them," Keturah corrected.

Her older sister gasped. "You must not say such prideful things," Grace scolded. "It displeases Gött."

"It looks like this little one is getting perfect care," Liz said. "I must go now though. I have an inn full of guests to take care of."

After Liz said good-bye to Miriam, the girls called out, "*Auf wiedersen.*"

As Liz drove to the inn, she pondered the story Miriam had told her. It was difficult for her to feel too bad for Nora. The woman had taken another Amish girl with her, then dumped her when her plan to marry someone out of the community was complete. That kind of selfishness seemed right in line with the woman Liz had met at the courthouse.

Thankfully, there were no crises when Liz returned to the inn, but she barely had time to set out the lemon bars and beverages for the coffee hour. All the guests turned up for it, which was unusual for a summer afternoon with so many local activities going on.

As Liz passed around the plate of lemon squares, Brya grabbed one and took a big bite, raining powdered sugar onto her bright pink T-shirt. Her mother tutted over the mess, but the little girl merely looked up at Liz and asked, "Did you find out who owns the little gem?"

"Brya," her mother scolded, "not with your mouth full."

"I haven't found the owner yet," Liz said, "but I also haven't forgotten you want it."

"Are you giving away gems?" Jessica asked as she took a lemon square of her own. "And can I get on the list to receive one?"

Liz chuckled. "If I start handing out gems, I'll let you know. I found a pretty green crystal. I assume it fell off someone's purse, or maybe it's a jacket embellishment. I honestly don't know where it came from."

"Can I see it?" Jessica asked.

"It's in my room," Liz said. "I'll try to remember to bring it to breakfast. Especially since someone is awfully eager to get it if I don't find its real home."

Brya nodded enthusiastically.

The rest of the coffee hour went well. No one brought up the snake scare, which Liz appreciated, though she was fairly certain she heard Gwen ask Brya something about snakes at one point while Liz was listening to another dream story from Harriet. The conversation between Gwen and the child didn't turn accusatory, so Liz soon relaxed and tuned in to what Harriet was saying, which involved balloons and an elephant.

After cleaning up from the coffee hour, Liz was happy to retire to her quarters, intending to see if she could get at least partway through the book she'd taken to the courthouse. She curled up on the comfy love seat and was soon immersed in the book, sloughing off tension from the day with each turn of the page.

Eventually, Liz closed the book and glanced out the windows, surprised to see total darkness pressing against them. She hadn't realized how many hours had passed. She rushed around the inn, locking up for the night, and then she crawled into bed, ready for a much more normal day in the morning.

Unfortunately, she didn't make it to morning. After only a couple of hours, she was awakened by Beans barking wildly somewhere. She hopped up and pulled on a robe before hurrying out of her room to track down the dog.

Beans stood guard in the four-season room near the door that led outside, growling and barking. The sounds coming from the little dog's barrel chest made him sound much bigger and far more dangerous than he really was.

"What are you barking at?" Liz asked as she leaned close to the glass in the door. All she saw beyond was darkness.

Beans wiggled his back end to make his stubby tail wag and barked again at the door.

"Fine," she said. "We'll go out and see what has you all worked up."

She went to the kitchen and grabbed his leash from the hook on the wall, then snapped it on and led the dog outside, expecting to find that raccoons had been in the trash can again. But Beans half-dragged her around the yard, circling the house more than once and snuffling the bushes while growling. No raccoons turned up and neither did anything else.

Finally, Liz hauled the reluctant dog toward the door. "Come on. There's nothing out here but bugs and darkness."

Beans offered her a single deep bark, then seemed to give in and walked the rest of the way into the house without protest.

She unsnapped his leash and hung it back up, pointing at him as she did. "No more barking."

Beans wagged his tail with such vigor that he was soon exhausted and collapsed to the floor for a nap.

Liz shook her head, not really upset with him, and returned to her quarters. She opened the door and gasped. Her room was a complete mess. Someone had been inside.

She quietly backed out and closed the door, not knowing if the intruder was still in there. Her cell phone was near her bed, so she dashed to the kitchen and called the police from the landline. Then she stood outside her quarters and stared nervously at the door until the sound of someone pounding on the outside door nearly made her jump out of her skin.

After Liz calmed down enough to realize that intruders don't normally knock, she found Officer Jack Gerst waiting at the back door of the utility room. The young man's open, friendly face immediately made her feel better. "Dispatch told me you had an intruder?"

Liz swung the door wide open. "In my quarters. I'll show you."

"Is anything missing?" he asked as he followed her.

"I don't know. I was afraid to go in there, in case someone was still there." Liz explained how she had been awakened by the dog's barking and then discovered the room wrecked after coming back inside with Beans.

Officer Gerst's gaze turned toward the bulldog sprawled on the floor. "If the dog doesn't think there's anyone inside, there probably isn't."

"I didn't consider that," she admitted. "When I realized a stranger had been in my personal space, I was too shocked to think clearly."

"I can understand," he said, giving her a sympathetic look. "Let me walk around. Then I'll need you to tell me if anything is missing."

They looked carefully through the rooms of her quarters, which consisted of a small living room, a bedroom, and a bathroom. Though Liz lacked Sarah's passion for cleaning excellence, she still kept her quarters neat, and it was upsetting to see her things thrown on the floor and drawers pulled out. She had to clasp her hands together to resist the urge to rush around and start straightening up while the officer was searching for clues.

In her kitchenette, the door to the microwave hung open, but the really annoying part was the mini fridge. Not only was the door open, but half the contents were tossed on the floor. "That's just mean," she complained. "Who stores valuables in with the coffee creamer and cheese?"

"You'd be surprised," Officer Gerst answered. "Some people store their valuables in foil-wrapped packages in their freezers, so it's the first place many criminals check."

"Well, I don't," Liz grumbled. "Can I go ahead and clean it? I don't want my creamer to spoil, whatever is left in the carton. And if I don't wipe it off the floor, my living room is going to smell like spoiled milk."

Officer Gerst stepped out of her way. "Sure, but then we need to finish looking for what the intruder has stolen, assuming you find all your cheese still there."

She gave him a wry look and hurried to the bathroom for a damp cloth to mop up the creamer. As she passed through the bedroom, she felt a growl building in her chest at the sight of her clothes hanging out of the drawers of her dresser.

Once she had the mess from the fridge cleaned up, they continued the assessment of her personal belongings. It didn't take too long. Liz lived in the most valuable thing she owned, and she wasn't much of a hoarder because she'd been raised by a formerly Amish mother.

Finally, Liz stood in the bedroom next to the young officer and tried to pretend her underclothes weren't scattered on the floor. "I can't find a single thing missing. I have a few valuable handbags, but they're all here. My jewelry was dumped on the dresser, but not one piece is gone. And my laptop is still on the dresser where I left it. It's a good laptop. Wouldn't that be the logical item to steal?"

Before Officer Gerst could respond, she had an unlikely thought. Right in the middle of the dresser was one item that *looked* untouched, a tiny china box that her godson had given her for her birthday the first year he'd come to live with her. The box was exactly where it belonged, and the lid was on it. The very neatness of it made it appear out of place in the messy room. "Wait . . ."

Liz walked over to the dresser and lifted the lid on the box. It was empty, which normally wouldn't be odd as the box was too small to store anything. But yesterday Liz had put the little green crystal into the box for safekeeping. "I know what the intruder was after," she announced.

"Great." Officer Gerst joined her to peer into the empty box.

Liz explained discovering the small green crystal in her tote bag and not recognizing it. "I assumed I'd come across it around the inn. When things get hectic, finding something like that and picking it up would be an automatic gesture. Plus, I don't use that bag very often, so it could have been in there for months."

"If you don't use that bag often, why were you looking in it?" Officer Gerst asked.

"I'd taken it to the courthouse. I had jury duty, and I needed a big enough bag to carry a book in. When I got home I went through the bag because I always clean out my totes and purses before I store them."

"That means you got the gem at the courthouse," Officer Gerst said. "It was the only place you went since you last cleaned out the bag."

"Well, yes, maybe. But the crystal was small. I mean, it was big if it had been a real emerald, but it was still small enough that it could have gotten caught up in the lining of the bag when I cleaned it out. I'm sure I would have remembered if I picked up something at the courthouse. Also, the jury rooms weren't that clean. I wouldn't have been collecting things I found on the floor."

He shrugged. "Someone broke into your room to take the crystal. Perhaps that person believed it was an emerald. I assume it would be very valuable if it was real."

"Yes, an emerald that large would be worth a fortune. Unlike diamonds, emeralds are actually rare. But it's unlikely for anyone to run across a loose emerald of that size on a floor somewhere. It would have been ten karats at the bare minimum."

"So, it would have been worth, what? A couple thousand?"

"More like over $100,000."

Officer Gerst stared at her.

Then Liz had a frightening thought. She remembered Nora

bumping into her in the lounge. What if the woman had dropped the gem into her tote, intending to retrieve it later? What if it was the reason someone murdered her?

Had Liz been carrying around the key to the murder all this time?

11

As Liz told Officer Gerst her theory about a possible connection between the emerald and the murder of Nora Wexler, she began to doubt the idea. It sounded a little too James Bond when she said it out loud.

"Why would someone drop a gem into your bag?" he asked. "It sounds like a good way to lose a $100,000."

"Maybe she intended to steal my bag when we got outside," Liz said hesitantly.

Officer Gerst arched a brow but remained silent.

"You know, mug me or something," Liz quickly added. But even as she said it, she couldn't quite picture the woman from the courthouse as the mugging type. For one thing, her high-heeled shoes wouldn't have enabled her to make a quick getaway.

"I can make note of that possibility," Officer Gerst said, though his tone of voice suggested he'd rather not.

"Thank you."

"It's not like I have any other theories. Someone took advantage of your absence from your room to break in. And they stole your gem." He held out his notepad. "Could you draw a picture of the crystal for me? Showing the size and shape?"

Liz drew an oval, using light lines to suggest the facets. "The green was very intense," she said as she handed back the notepad. "Whether the gem was real or not, it certainly was pretty."

Officer Gerst glanced down at her drawing, then looked around the room. "Maybe the person stole it because it appeared potentially valuable."

"In that case, there were several other items that would have been more of a sure thing," Liz said. "I have a pair of diamond earrings that are fairly valuable, over $1,000 anyway. Again, a few of my purses are designer pieces, and they're in excellent condition and could draw a few hundred." She shrugged. "And like I said, my laptop wasn't taken either. I could understand if someone snatched the gem along with those other things."

"The gem would be the easiest to conceal," he said, "if the person is in the inn. Did anyone here know you had it?"

Liz laughed lightly. "Everyone here knows I had it. I was showing it around and trying to find the owner. I figured it was part of someone's purse decoration or maybe a piece on a jacket. Embellishments like that aren't uncommon in those kinds of applications."

"But no one showed any special interest," he said.

"Not unless you count an eight-year-old girl," Liz said. Then she froze. Brya had been extremely upset that Liz wouldn't give her the gem, and she had already gone into Davidia's room and taken her snake.

"I can see you have an idea," Officer Gerst said.

Liz didn't want to accuse the child. "I may, but if so, it's something I need to handle on my own."

"That's fine," he said, slipping his notepad into his pocket. "I'll fill out a report, and when you have a chance, you can stop by the station to look it over and sign it. His expression turned apologetic. "But I doubt we'll find a little green crystal. Even if it was a real gem, it's too easy to conceal and get rid of."

"I understand." Liz got the impression that Officer Gerst wasn't taking her break-in very seriously. Now that she suspected the culprit might be Brya, she wasn't taking it as seriously either, though she was definitely annoyed.

After showing the police officer out, Liz set about putting her quarters in order. It wouldn't leave her much time for sleep, but there was no way she could go to bed with all her belongings strewn across the floor. She was glad to see that the creamer was the only casualty of the intruder's visit. All the fragile items on her dresser and on the shelves in the living room remained intact.

"I'll take my good news where I can get it," she mumbled.

When everything was straightened up and put away, she dragged Beans into her living room. "You're on guard duty," she told him.

The dog licked her hand agreeably, then flopped down on the rug in front of the love seat and promptly started snoring.

"My hero." Liz headed off to bed, expecting to toss and turn, but apparently Beans was hero enough to set her mind at ease. She slept deeply until her alarm woke her with a start.

When she got up, she carried her laptop to the kitchen, intending to grab a moment after breakfast to try an Internet search on Nora. Liz was sure that either Brya had played another trick or the break-in was somehow related to the woman's death since it didn't make any sense as a robbery.

Who would break into the B&B in order to steal a small embellishment crystal?

Suddenly, Liz had a thought. What if she'd picked up something that identified the killer somehow? Her imagination supplied the image of a fight in the elevator between Nora and some gem-bedazzled assailant carrying bees around. Nora could have torn the crystal from the attacker's clothes. And when Liz caught Nora outside the elevator, the crystal fell out of Nora's hand and into Liz's bag.

Liz shook her head. She couldn't exactly put much faith into her vision of a bedazzled killer, and the whole idea of a piece of evidence tumbling into Liz's bag seemed far-fetched.

"Never brainstorm when sleep-deprived," she muttered. Then she decided to turn her attention to something truly productive: coffee.

Preparing breakfast was more of a challenge than usual, but a hot cup of coffee helped clear her fuzzy head enough to avoid cutting herself as she sliced fresh fruit to go along with the granola, yogurt, and a pile of toast made from locally baked bread. Liz knew from experience that the guests appreciated lighter breakfasts full of local ingredients in the summer, so she restricted her morning meat to some prosciutto tucked into sliced melon.

Over breakfast, Liz kept an eye on Brya, watching for signs of guilt on the little girl's face. She concluded that the child was an amazing actress or she was innocent. Of course, Liz hadn't seen any guilty looks when Brya was hiding a snake in her room either. However, she noticed that the child didn't ask about the emerald even once. Considering how much she'd pestered Liz about it, that lack of interest was suspicious in itself.

Liz was so distracted by her study of Brya during breakfast that Harriet had to ask her twice about where Liz got the flowers for the rooms.

"Oh, forgive me. I didn't sleep very well last night," Liz responded. "The flowers are from the gardens right here."

"How nice. Did you arrange them?"

"I wish I could take credit for that, but Kiera Williams does the arranging." Kiera was Liz's other part-time employee. The teen had a way with flowers and plants, and she was responsible for placing the bouquets of fresh flowers in the guest rooms.

"I'll have to tell her how much I love the flowers," Harriet said.

"She doesn't work today," Liz said, "but I'm sure she'll be around tomorrow."

Gwen leaned forward from across the table. "You mentioned not sleeping well. Was it the dog? I heard him barking not long after I went to bed."

"His barking was part of it," Liz said. "I'm sorry if he kept you awake."

Gwen waved it off. "He didn't bark long. He seemed terribly upset, but then a squirrel can cause a dog to act like the house is under siege. I wasn't really bothered, only mildly curious, and I fell asleep the second he stopped."

Liz felt a surge of relief. "Beans is normally a quiet dog."

"That's obvious. If he was any quieter, I would think he was a stuffed toy," Harriet said. "Yesterday Sadie was telling me what a great watchdog he is. I guess last night he proved it."

"Beans is like a ninja," Brya announced loyally, which surprised Liz since Brya had said the dog was boring the last time his name had come up. "Silent and unnoticed until he's needed."

Liz laughed. "A ninja is one comparison I've never thought of with Beans. You might not either if you'd ever heard him snore."

After breakfast, Liz managed to get the dishes cleared and the kitchen cleaned up before anything troubling happened. She was drying her hands on one of the soft, striped kitchen towels when she heard a knock at the back door. *I'm beginning to develop a phobia of that sound*, she thought as she walked through the utility room and saw Chief Houghton at the door.

"You just missed breakfast," Liz said as she let him in, "but I still have some coffee on."

"I'll gladly take the coffee," the chief replied as he followed Liz to the kitchen. He stood quietly while she fixed him a mug of coffee, then said, "I heard about your intruder."

"And you came for that?" Liz handed him the mug. "I'm touched."

"Actually, your gem likely ties into Ms. Wexler's murder."

Liz gaped at him. "Really? I already entertained the idea, but it seemed too hard to believe."

Chief Houghton took a deep sip of his coffee. "Truth is stranger than fiction. It turns out that Ms. Wexler was in the middle of a huge row with her ex-husband, Will."

"*That* I heard in the jury room."

He gestured slightly with his cup. "But the focus of the brouhaha was an emerald engagement ring. It was a Wexler family heirloom and featured a ten-karat oval emerald. This emerald had no enhancements, which didn't mean much to me, but apparently it means a good deal when you're talking about emeralds. They're rare and valuable, especially in an emerald of that color and clarity. The family said the gem alone was worth well over $100,000."

"The gem I found wasn't in a ring," Liz reminded him. "It was loose."

"The setting was a big deal too," the chief said. "It was made by a high-end jewelry designer who was related to the family somehow. The designer has been dead for over fifty years, and his work has skyrocketed in value since then. This emerald engagement ring was a special piece. So special that it's become something like an emblem for the family."

"An emblem?"

"Yes, it's in wills and everything. The oldest son of each generation inherits the engagement ring, but only if his mother was a legal wife who wore it. If there is no heir who fits that role, all the Wexler family money is turned into a charitable foundation and no one inherits. It sounds strange, but I guess it's legal."

"Wow," Liz said softly. "How much money are we talking about?"

"Millions," Chief Houghton stated. "So, anyway, when Will and Nora Wexler divorced, she was supposed to hand over the ring, but she wouldn't. She said an engagement ring was a gift, and it belonged to her. Finally, a judge ordered her to turn over the ring. But something about the wording of the court order gave her a loophole, and she only turned over the setting. She kept the gem."

"That must have upset her ex-husband and his family."

He nodded. "You know it. Especially since he's planning to remarry, and he needs that ring. Without it, his heirs will be out in the cold. I was told it might count with a different gem since it's the same setting, but the family doesn't want to risk it with the value of the estate. They wanted Ms. Wexler to return the gem. She insisted that she'd lost it, but no one believed her."

"So the gem in my tote bag was the emerald from the ring. I was carrying around an emerald worth over $100,000 in my shirt pocket." The thought nearly made her dizzy. "I imagine this puts Will Wexler at the top of the suspect list."

"Normally, it would," he agreed, "especially since Mr. Wexler was near the courthouse on the day Nora died, but he was at his attorney's office. They spent the morning outlining some conditions for a prenuptial agreement for the new pending Mrs. Wexler. I guess he learned a few things from his first wife."

"There's no way he could have slipped away?" Liz asked.

The chief shrugged. "His lawyer and several people in the lawyer's office say no, and Mr. Wexler says he had no idea his ex-wife was going to be at the courthouse." He smiled. "Now I'm going to look into where he was last night when the emerald vanished from your room."

"He'd have no way of knowing the gem was here," Liz said. "I didn't even know it was here. Nora didn't exactly announce that she was going to hide the emerald in my tote. And why would she do that anyway?"

"It does sound crazy, but from what I've learned, the Wexler woman was prone to unusual behavior."

"Still, it was risky behavior," Liz said. "Why go to so much effort to keep the emerald, only to hand it off to a stranger?"

"Maybe it was the ultimate insult to the Wexlers," Chief Houghton suggested. "Ms. Wexler must have known they'd legally get the gem away from her eventually, and she wanted to stick it to the ex, so she simply passed it off to a stranger. It might have been a spur-of-the-moment decision."

"Maybe," Liz replied, though she still wasn't at all sure. "You know, I might have a possible suspect in the gem theft a little closer to home." She told Chief Houghton about showing the emerald around to all the guests and how adamant Brya was about getting the gem. "She didn't know it was real, of course, but she's a very determined child."

"Maybe we should chat with her," Chief Houghton said. "And her mother, of course."

As Liz had feared, Courtney was not exactly thrilled to have her daughter suspected of theft again. "My daughter believed you when you said she would get the crystal if you didn't find the owner. Brya had no reason to take it. She's not a thief."

"She took Miss Burke's snake," Liz said as calmly as she was able, "and she put it into another guest's room as a prank. So we've already determined that she's quite capable of taking things that are not hers."

"I didn't take Cleopatra," Brya yelled. "I borrowed her." At the look of shock on her mother's face, she dropped her volume. "Cleopatra liked being in my dresser drawer. I could tell. I petted her every day. And I would have given her back, but that other lady was mean to me."

Courtney frowned at her daughter. "That doesn't make your prank okay. You know that. We talked about it."

Brya stuck out her lower lip. "I still didn't steal Cleopatra. The snake lady got her back. I only borrowed her."

Chief Houghton smiled at the child. "Did you borrow the crystal from Miss Eckardt's room?"

Brya shook her head, but she didn't speak. She only glared with her lower lip still out.

"Did you mess up Miss Eckardt's rooms looking for the crystal?" Chief Houghton asked. "I could understand it if you did. You thought of it as yours."

"It wasn't mine yet," Brya said.

"But it was promised to you," the chief coaxed. "That's almost like being yours."

"If I did take the crystal, I wouldn't mess up anything," Brya said.

"I didn't mess up Miss Burke's room when I got Cleopatra. And I didn't take the crystal."

"Brya, I expect you to tell the truth," her mother said firmly.

"I am telling the truth." Brya stamped her foot. "I didn't take it." Then she admitted quietly, "But I might know who did."

Chief Houghton and Liz exchanged looks. "I'm listening," he said.

Brya smirked at them. "I'll tell you if you give me a present."

"I'll give you a present, young lady," her mother said. "I'll take away all your electronics for a month if you don't tell the police chief what he wants to know."

Brya turned to her mother, her face a mask of shock and alarm. "Okay, I was going to tell anyway."

"So tell," Liz said.

"Mom takes a sleeping pill at night," Brya said.

Her mother rolled her eyes. "Stick to what you know about the crystal."

"It's part of the story," Brya protested.

With another eye roll that made her look surprisingly like her daughter, Courtney said, "Fine, just tell the story."

"She uses earplugs too," the little girl added.

"Brya." Her mother's tone had a warning edge.

Brya locked eyes with her mother, then dropped her gaze. "Mom was sleeping," she said after a moment, "but I couldn't fall asleep. I tried counting sheep, but that never works."

"It never works for me either," Chief Houghton said supportively.

"I know, right?" Brya said. "I don't get why people even talk about it. Anyway, I took out my flashlight and was reading *Freckles* under the covers, but I got hot."

"Understandable," Chief Houghton said, and Liz marveled at his patience.

"So I decided to go slide down the banister."

Liz looked at the child in horror and noticed a matching expression on Courtney's face. "That's dangerous. Please tell me you didn't actually do it."

"Not last night," Brya responded, which didn't make Liz feel much better. "I couldn't slide because someone was coming down the stairs from up there." She pointed at the ceiling.

"You're sure?" Liz asked. "Did you see the person?"

Brya shook her head. "I hid back in our room. Then I heard Beans barking a whole bunch, and I sneaked out to see why. I went downstairs, and I saw someone run by the windows in the library."

"Someone was in the library?" Chief Houghton said.

"No, I was in the library. Someone was outside in the bushes near the windows."

"That must have been who Beans was barking at," Liz said.

Brya shrugged. "I walked around downstairs, looking out the windows. Then I heard you taking Beans out for a walk. I thought maybe he would find me when you came back in, so I went upstairs."

"And you never saw the person who came down the stairs?" Chief Houghton asked.

"No, but I heard them run upstairs after I was in my room," Brya answered. "I bet that person took the crystal. You should make them give it back so I can have it."

"I'm sorry, Brya," Chief Houghton said, "but Liz can't give you the crystal. I found out who it really belongs to."

"Oh, that stinks," Brya said.

"But you were very helpful."

"Do I get a reward?" Brya asked.

"Not likely," her mother replied. "What you're going to get is a good grounding."

At that, Brya flopped dramatically onto the bed.

Chief Houghton thanked them both for their help and led Liz out of the room. "We'll have to talk to all your guests on the third floor."

Liz smiled. "That will be easy. I have only one guest on the third floor."

"Great. Let's go arrest a jewel thief."

12

The stairs to the third floor were steeper and narrower than the sweeping staircase that led to the second floor. When Liz had first taken over the bed-and-breakfast, she thought the third-floor staircase was too dark and a little creepy so she added more lights.

As she followed Chief Houghton up the stairs, she still felt uneasy. The feeling wasn't lessened when he insisted that Liz stay behind him. "You're the civilian," he reminded her, "and I'm the one with the gun."

"I doubt you're going to need a gun. Jessica Ellis doesn't really strike me as being very dangerous."

"Those are the ones who can do the most damage," the chief said. "Ask me sometime to tell you about the little old lady who killed an intruder with a knitting needle."

Liz winced. "Actually, I'd rather you didn't tell me about that. Ever."

He chuckled. "As you wish."

The third-floor landing was considerably smaller than the landing on the second floor because the slope of the inn's roof took up a significant amount of space. Several of the doors along the walls were kept locked as they led only to storage rooms with low ceilings. As a result, the space on the third floor was either cozy or claustrophobic, depending on your mood. Usually, Liz found it cozy. Today she wasn't so sure.

"Which room?" Chief Houghton whispered. Liz pointed to the Sunset Room, and he knocked firmly on the door.

The door cracked open, and Jessica peeked out. Her black hair was pulled up in a messy twist with a few tendrils falling around her face. She also had glasses perched on her nose.

The change in her appearance startled Liz. Before Jessica could speak, Liz finally realized why the young woman had seemed so familiar when she arrived at the inn. Jessica resembled a younger version of the dark-haired woman who'd given Nora such a vicious look in the jury waiting room.

Jessica gave the chief's uniform a nervous once-over. "Can I help you?" she asked before turning back into the room and shouting, "Pixie, sit!"

"May we come in?" Chief Houghton asked.

Jessica hesitated, then opened the door while using her bare foot to keep her dog from rushing through the crack. She was wearing a long T-shirt and yoga pants, the same thing she'd worn to breakfast, and there were dark smudges under her eyes, which Liz hadn't noticed at the breakfast table.

Liz and the chief entered the room, and the fluffy little dog danced around their feet, tail wagging.

"Calm down, Pixie," Jessica scolded, nudging the dog farther from Liz and Chief Houghton. "She's really very friendly, but I can put her in her carrier if you'd like. I know she can be distracting."

"Pixie's fine. I like dogs." The chief bent and rubbed the dog's ears.

Pixie rewarded him with a deluge of licking.

"How can I help you?" Jessica asked.

Chief Houghton stood up and removed a notebook from his pocket. "I'm investigating an incident that occurred at the inn last night around midnight. Someone entered Miss Eckardt's private quarters, ransacked them, and stole something from her dresser."

"How horrible," Jessica said. She gave Liz a distressed look. "Do you often have break-ins here? I thought this was a safe place."

"It wasn't really a break-in," Liz said with a grim smile. "Apparently, it was a guest."

Chief Houghton gave Liz a quelling gaze. Clearly, he wanted to handle the interrogation. "Miss Ellis, is that your real name?"

"Of course it's my real name," Jessica said. "What are you implying?"

The chief scrawled on his pad without answering her for a moment, then looked up and gave her a calm stare. "I'm not implying anything, just gathering facts. For instance, it is a fact that you're not as surprised by the incident last night as you pretend."

"I beg your pardon!" She glared at him.

"Miss Ellis, we have an eyewitness. One of the guests downstairs doesn't sleep much, and she was very curious about your comings and goings."

Jessica's face visibly paled. "Oh." She stepped away from Liz and the chief until the backs of her legs bumped into a nearby chair, and then she sat down. "You have to understand that I *had* to get the gem." She straightened up slightly and attempted a defiant tone, but her voice was too shaky to pull it off. "I didn't do anything wrong."

"Are you a member of the Wexler family?" the chief asked.

"No. Not yet. Actually, I guess I won't ever be really." Jessica stopped and held up her hand while she took a couple of deep, calming breaths. When she started speaking again, her rush of words made it clear that the breathing hadn't helped much. "My sister is Rebecca Ellis. She's engaged to Will Wexler. Well, sort of engaged. The engagement won't be recognized by the Wexler family until she can wear the Wexler emerald. But they are in love, and they intend to be married as soon as they recover the Wexler emerald. I was simply helping with that." She turned to Liz. "You had the emerald in your room, but it rightfully belongs to my sister or, rather, to the Wexlers and then my sister."

"How did you find out I had the emerald?" Liz asked. "I didn't show it to you. I'd already put it in my room."

"You mentioned it at the coffee hour," Jessica said. "My sister thought you might have it when it didn't turn up in Nora's belongings or at her house."

The chief's expression sharpened. "How did you know the emerald wasn't at Ms. Wexler's house?"

Jessica swallowed. "My sister and I looked. The police had already been there. The neighbors said so. That means we weren't disturbing anything you hadn't already seen."

"That doesn't stop it from being breaking and entering," the chief said, "and interfering with an investigation."

"Yes, fine, my sister and I did some things we probably shouldn't have, but you have to understand that Nora *stole* the gem," Jessica said, her voice shaking. "The ring has been important to the Wexlers for generations. It's more than an heirloom. It's part of their identity. Nora lost her right to it when she and Will split up. She was horrible to him."

"You forgot to mention that the emerald is key to the family inheritance," Chief Houghton said.

"Oh, you know about that?" Jessica's voice shook even more.

"Yes, ma'am," the chief answered. "So why did you come to this inn? I'll assume it wasn't a wild coincidence."

Jessica shook her head, causing more strands of her black hair to fall from the loose twist. "My sister has been following Nora around, and I've helped when I could." She faced Liz. "Anyway, Rebecca was in the jury waiting room with you and Nora. She had a line of sight from the waiting area to the lounge. She saw Nora bump into you. Later, when we were desperate about the jewel, she remembered the incident and thought Nora might have passed you the gem. As it turned out, she was right."

"Nora apparently dropped it into my tote bag," Liz replied. "I found it later, but I had no idea how I came by it. And I still have no idea why Nora would do something like that."

"We decided she must have recognized Rebecca," Jessica said. "We thought Nora had no idea who Will planned to marry, but that's the only thing we can figure out. She recognized Rebecca and didn't want a confrontation with the emerald on her person. She knew she had no right to it—although I can't imagine why she'd even have it with her at jury duty."

"So, was there a confrontation?" Chief Houghton asked Jessica.

"No, Rebecca was only following her."

"How did she get into the jury waiting room?" Liz inquired. "Surely, she didn't have jury duty, and you have to sign in to get inside."

Jessica waved a hand. "Rebecca said the jury clerk wasn't paying attention, so she simply walked in and snagged a sticker from the podium. Then she acted like she belonged there, and no one questioned it."

"Where is the gem now?" the chief asked.

Jessica dropped her gaze to her hands. "My sister has it."

"How did you get it to her so fast?" Liz asked. From the corner of her eye, she noticed Chief Houghton frowning at her, but she ignored him.

"She was outside the inn last night," Jessica explained. "She walked through the bushes until your dog started barking."

"How did you know he would bark?" Liz asked. Upon first meeting, Beans didn't exactly look like the watchdog type. He looked more like the "lay on the floor until you trip over him" type.

"I went to the quilt shop downstairs yesterday," Jessica said, "and the white-haired lady . . ."

"Sadie," Liz suggested.

Jessica shot her a grateful smile. "Sadie was telling someone what a great watchdog Beans can be. The other person didn't believe it, so Sadie provided examples. And that gave me the idea for how I could get into your quarters. Rebecca thrashed in the bushes. Then when you went outside, I looked for the emerald in your room. When I found it, I passed it to Rebecca through one of the downstairs windows before I ran back to my room."

"An elaborate plan," the chief said. "It sounds like you and your sister are fond of elaborate plans. How long did it take you to cook up the scheme to kill Ms. Wexler with the beestings? It must have been disappointing when your sister couldn't find the emerald on Ms. Wexler after the attack."

Jessica stared at him in wide-eyed horror. "My sister didn't hurt Nora. We wanted the gem, but we wouldn't hurt anyone to get it."

Chief Houghton closed his notebook and slid it into his pocket. "You'll have to forgive me if I doubt that. After all, your sister has millions of reasons to commit murder to get that gem—the Wexler millions. I have seen murder committed with a much weaker motive than that."

Jessica whispered, "You're wrong. We wouldn't harm anyone, not even Nora."

"But you'll understand that I'll be taking you down to the station," Chief Houghton said. "At the very least, you broke into Miss Eckardt's quarters and stole something from her room."

"Something that didn't belong to her," Jessica protested. "She knew it didn't belong to her, or she wouldn't have been trying to find the owner."

"Right. I was trying to find the owner. That means you could have asked for it anytime," Liz pointed out. "You heard me trying to find the rightful owner. Why not simply ask for it?"

"I thought about it, but Rebecca said we shouldn't. If we admitted how much the emerald was worth, she thought you might act like Nora. Then we'd be back where we started but with a different person."

"Miss Eckardt would not have been allowed to hang on to stolen property even if she was the sort to do so," Chief Houghton said.

"Which I'm not," Liz interjected.

He turned his mild gaze toward her, the corner of his mouth quirking up. "Which she's not." His tone was serious as he continued, "Your sister was wrong. I believe I'll be inviting her down to the station for a talk too. Right now, you'll be coming with me, and I'll send someone to bring your sister to us."

Jessica looked at Liz, her expression pleading. "I know you don't have any reason to do me any favors, but would you please take care of

Pixie until I can come back for her? She hates being left alone."

Liz glanced down at the fluffy little dog who sat on the floor at Jessica's feet, gazing up at her mistress intently. "I'll take care of Pixie. Don't worry about that."

Jessica managed a watery smile. "Thank you. You're a good person. I'm sorry about rifling through your things."

Liz shrugged. "You didn't break anything. I could have done without the spilled creamer though."

Jessica cringed. "Yes, that was an accident."

"This is all very touching," Chief Houghton interrupted, "but we need to get going. I have a murder to solve."

Opting to skip the handcuffs, he led the downcast woman out of the inn, and Liz followed with Pixie in her arms. At the door, he allowed Jessica to give the little dog a quick hug.

"Pixie will be fine," Liz assured her.

Appearing scared but resolute, Jessica left with the chief.

Liz stood staring out the front window at the street, absently petting the dog in her arms. She staggered a step when she felt a hard bump against her right leg. She glanced down to see Beans, panting happily and wagging half his body as he looked up adoringly at the dog she was holding.

Pixie peered over Liz's arm and gave a sharp yap.

"I do hope you're not going to be a yappy dog after all," she admonished.

Pixie wriggled in her arms until Liz was concerned she might drop the little dog. She set Pixie on the floor and watched her sniff noses with Beans. In moments, the two dogs were racing around the foyer, much to Liz's surprise, considering Beans was usually more of a slightly smelly ornament than a lively pet.

"I'm glad you two are happy."

She turned her attention back to the window. She believed Jessica's story about her sister and the Wexler emerald. Jessica didn't seem like a killer, though Liz knew from experience that killers didn't always appear evil.

Liz felt goose bumps on her arms. As she rubbed them away, she realized her instincts were telling her that Nora's killer was still out there somewhere.

13

Liz was still staring distractedly out the front window, barely registering what was right in front of her, when she realized someone was walking up the steps to the porch. The person stopped on the other side of the window and pecked on it with one finger, making Liz smile.

Naomi held up a white box. "I come bearing gifts." As always, the owner of Sweet Everything looked lovely. She wore a pale green flowered blouse, and her wild curls were pulled back into a low ponytail.

Liz opened the front door for her friend. "You'd be welcome with or without gifts."

"But with gifts is always better." Naomi grinned as she entered. "I'm experimenting with new tartlets made with local berries, and I thought I'd bring you some for your coffee hour."

Liz took the box and gave Naomi a one-armed hug. "You're an angel of mercy. I appreciate not having to bake after the morning I've experienced. Do you have time for a cup of coffee?"

"After that mysterious greeting, of course," Naomi said as they walked through the inn. "I assume your life has gotten more exciting since we last spoke."

"Exciting, confusing, frustrating, slightly terrifying," Liz said, ticking them off on her fingers.

When they reached the kitchen, she waved Naomi toward the breakfast nook and poured them mugs of coffee. When she handed Naomi her mug and dropped into a seat, she was amazed at how glad she was to see her friend. "It's been a tough few days. Starting with my morning of jury duty."

"You drank the coffee, didn't you?" Naomi chided.

"Yes, and you were right. But that turned out to be one of the nicer parts of the day." Liz sighed. "Did you hear about the woman who died at the courthouse?"

Naomi took a sip of her coffee and nodded. "Did you know her?"

"Not before that day," Liz said. "Nora Wexler was there for jury duty, right up until they sent us all home and she practically died in my arms." At Naomi's confused expression, she slowed down and went through the details of her morning at the courthouse in a more orderly way.

"That sounds horrible," Naomi said when Liz finished. "I've never seen anyone have an allergic reaction like that. It must have been scary."

"In that I wasn't sure what to do, yes, it was," Liz admitted. "But I don't doubt it was much more terrifying for her."

"Terrifying and clearly disorienting. Otherwise, why would the woman accuse you of trying to kill her?"

"I don't know," Liz said. "Though it may have been related to the emerald Nora slipped into my tote bag. Maybe she was trying to draw attention to me because of that."

Naomi's eyes widened. "Emerald in your tote bag? Way to bury the lead. What on earth happened?"

Liz managed a mirthless laugh. "I found a little green crystal in my tote bag and thought it was an embellishment from someone's purse or jacket. I figured I'd picked it up around the inn, maybe even weeks or months ago, and I'd just forgotten about it. So I've been showing off this emerald worth $100,000 and asking people if they lost it."

Naomi laughed. "Any takers?"

"Only the eight-year-old I have staying here," Liz said. "But as it turned out, one of my guests did want it, so Jessica broke into my quarters last night after having her sister, Rebecca, set Beans off by lurking in the bushes outside." Liz explained the importance of the Wexler emerald, Chief Houghton's questioning of Jessica, and Rebecca's presence in the jury waiting room. "The chief figures Jessica or her sister or both have a pretty strong motive for murder."

"It sure sounds like it." Naomi took a slow sip of coffee, watching Liz over the rim of the cup. "You don't believe the chief is right, do you?"

"I don't know, of course," Liz said. "But after listening to Jessica, I couldn't see her killing Nora or being involved in it either."

"Maybe her sister did it," Naomi said. "You said Rebecca looked furious at the courthouse. People have done worse things under the influence of anger."

"Yes," Liz agreed hesitantly.

"But you don't think so. Who do you suspect?"

"I don't have enough details, but I'm leaning toward the ex. Will's family has millions and he wants an heir, which he cannot have unless he gets the emerald back. Plus, Nora was obviously doing everything she could to make the man miserable. And he certainly would have known about her allergy since he was married to her."

Naomi set her mug on the table. "But I'm sure many people knew about it. From what you said, she was prone to telling others all about her business."

"Nora told people about how mistreated she was," Liz said, "but she didn't mention the allergy in the jury waiting room."

"Still, if Will has millions, couldn't he simply get a new gem for the ring? It seems like it would be the setting that really matters, and he has that."

"Maybe, but even though my area of law was patents, I've seen plenty of inheritance cases turn into vicious fights when that kind of money is involved. Someone might argue that putting in a new gem would make it a new ring, and thus, it wouldn't meet the demands of the family inheritance rules."

"But who would do that?" Naomi asked.

"Whoever is going to benefit from the massive outpouring of Wexler money if it becomes a charitable foundation. Charities can be big money." Liz set her mug down and stared into the swirling liquid. "When I was in college, I took a criminal law class, and my instructor said that when it came to murder, the smartest investigators will follow the money."

"Then the sisters are the most likely suspects, don't you think? Will is already going to inherit, assuming his mother wore the ring when she married."

Liz's gaze snapped up. "Actually, we don't know if she did. Maybe something stood in the way of that. What if one or both of Will's parents is alive, and he has to marry and have an heir so he can control the money for the heir? That would be a huge motive."

"And it would create many confusing what-ifs," Naomi said. "Plus, that doesn't change Rebecca's motive. If she marries Will, anything that benefits him will also benefit her." She added, "Didn't Chief Houghton tell you that Will had an alibi?"

Liz snorted. "Yes, given to him by his attorney. The law office isn't far from the courthouse. What if Will snuck away long enough to kill Nora? It's not like his lawyer wouldn't vouch for him, even if he had to lie."

Naomi raised her eyebrows. "Considering you practiced law for years, you seem to have a dim view of your fellow lawyers."

"That's *because* I practiced law for so many years."

Naomi reached out and patted Liz's hand. "I happen to know that not every lawyer is a money-hungry evildoer. I know one who is pretty terrific."

Liz smiled. "Thanks for the vote of confidence. Still, I have this nagging feeling that the chief isn't searching in the right place. He feels like he has his suspects. What if he's wrong, and what if he stops looking?"

"I'm beginning to suspect a plan brewing." Naomi drained the last of her coffee and set the mug down firmly. "Whatever it is, count me in."

Liz looked at her in surprise. "Really? Without hearing it?"

"I trust you," Naomi said, "and I welcome a little adventure now and then. I read a lot of Nancy Drew novels when I was a little girl. I'd love to play sleuth."

"Well, I'd like to drive to Nora's house and take a look at the place."

"You know where it is?"

"Chief Houghton told me. I don't think he imagined I'd go out there."

"How much do you suppose we'll learn by wandering around in the yard?"

"Jessica and Rebecca searched the house for the emerald," Liz said. "There must be a way in." At Naomi's startled expression, she added, "I'll probably just look in the windows, but if the sisters left a door hanging open . . ."

"They might have had a key."

Liz shook her head. "Nora wouldn't give her ex-husband's fiancée and her sister a house key. Besides, they didn't personally know Nora. I know because Jessica said that Rebecca never expected Nora to recognize her at the courthouse."

"Sound reasoning. Nancy Drew would be proud," Naomi said. "Let's go peek in the windows."

"You know we could get into trouble," Liz warned her.

Naomi laughed. "Now you're getting me excited."

They drove over to the big, worn Victorian. The house was gray with the trim painted an odd slate green. Though the trim was pretty, broken pieces above the front door and around the second-floor windows spoiled even that charm. A mismatched door had been added to the side turret, and a spindly fire escape crawled up the opposite side of the house.

"This place is a crime against remodeling," Naomi said as they pulled into the weed-choked driveway.

"It certainly doesn't look like Nora was living the high life," Liz commented. "Now we simply have to figure out what part of this monster held her apartment."

Name stickers on the mailboxes that lined the small porch gave them the information they needed. Nora had lived in most of the first floor. The turret comprised a townhome-style apartment, and the majority of the second floor made up a third apartment. The door to Nora's apartment was locked, but it didn't take much searching to find an open window with the screen partially raised as well.

"That window must be the way Jessica and her sister got in," Liz said. "And it's just hanging open. Who knows what could have crawled inside?"

"It's almost our civic duty to check," Naomi replied. "Who goes first?"

"It was my idea," Liz said. "I suppose I should take the plunge." Climbing through the window was fairly easy. She quickly wriggled through it, ending up in a sprawl on the floor below the window.

With Liz's help, Naomi was able to make a slightly more graceful entrance.

"It was nice of Nora not to put any furniture in front of the window," Naomi whispered cheerfully as she dusted off her knees.

A quick search didn't turn up much. The house was messy, which Liz found surprising. Nora had been raised Amish, so Liz expected her to have the kind of housecleaning ethic that she saw in Sarah, Miriam, and her own mother. Instead, Nora appeared to be very casual.

Liz stood in the middle of the living room and looked at a coffee table piled high with magazines, remote controls, mail, an empty coffee mug, and a wilted Christmas cactus. "Why do I feel the urge to water the plant?"

"Because you're kindhearted," Naomi said. "So, do we go through her mail?"

Liz leafed through the envelopes without opening them. They covered the basic utilities and a few magazine subscriptions. Nothing out of the ordinary.

"On to the bedroom?" Naomi asked.

Liz gestured for Naomi to lead the way, though she was feeling less and less like their trespassing was going to produce anything interesting. The bedroom was neater than the living room, and the old quilt that covered the bed appeared Amish, the first sign of Nora's past in the whole apartment. Then Liz found what she believed was the second sign: a single photo in a cheap frame perched on the mantel of the small fireplace.

Liz picked it up for a closer look. The photo showed Nora and another woman. Nora looked young, and Liz guessed the picture had been taken ten or fifteen years ago. Nora stared straight into the lens, laughing, but the second woman was blurry as she seemed to be trying to look away from the camera. All Liz could really tell about her was that she wore glasses and had pulled her hair back in a neat braid.

"Who is that?" Naomi asked.

"I wonder if this might be Nora's friend Prudence." Liz held out the photo so Naomi could see it better. "Miriam told me that Nora left the Amish community with a friend."

"It's too bad the photo is so blurry. You can hardly tell anything about the second woman other than her blond hair." Naomi leaned closer, squinting, then pointed with one finger. "Is that a birthmark on her neck?"

"I can't tell. It might be a shadow." Liz felt oddly reluctant to set the photo down.

"Let's check out the bathroom," Naomi suggested. "You can tell a lot about a woman by her toiletries."

"You can?" Liz asked.

"Absolutely. Come on and I'll demonstrate."

Still clutching the photo, Liz followed Naomi toward the far door. She glanced at the photo again and wondered if there was any way to track down Prudence. At one time, the woman had been very close to Nora. She might have some insights into Nora's marriage with Will and whether or not he was the kind of person who could kill his ex.

Naomi reached out to open the bathroom door, but instead, the door burst open on its own, slamming into Naomi and making her stumble backward into Liz.

A figure in black clothes and a dark ski mask tore out of the bathroom, both hands extended, fingers bent like claws.

14

The intruder struck Naomi, who was already off balance, sending her slamming hard into Liz. Together Liz and Naomi fell in a tangle. After a few stumbling steps, the intruder scrambled over them and rushed past.

Liz jumped to her feet and chased the stranger, but by the time she got to the living room, the intruder had already flung open the front door and fled.

She heard a chorus of "ouches" behind her and headed back to the bedroom where Naomi was using the side of the bed to haul herself awkwardly to her feet.

"Are you all right?" Liz asked, feeling guilty about abandoning her friend.

"I'll be fine in a minute," Naomi said. "I twisted my ankle a little. Did you see what hit us?"

Liz shook her head. "Other than someone in the basic burglar outfit? No." She sighed. "I think we're going to have to call the police. Chief Houghton will be thrilled with me. Do you want to leave now and avoid the hassle?"

"Hassled by the police?" Naomi managed a slightly pained smile. "Bring it on."

Since it seemed wrong to wait inside the house for the police to arrive, like flaunting their misbehavior, Liz and Naomi sat in a battered, crooked porch swing until a police car pulled into the driveway. Liz was glad to see Officer Gerst get out of the car. He waved at her.

"How are you still on duty?" she asked when he reached the porch. "Shouldn't you be home in bed?"

Officer Gerst nodded. "My whole body agrees that I should, but I'm piling on the overtime right now." His cheeks pinked slightly, and he grinned. "I'm saving up, so I can marry my girlfriend in the fall."

"Congratulations," Liz said. "She's a lucky girl."

"Thanks." The officer motioned to the front door and cleared his throat. "This is the house you broke into?"

"We didn't exactly break in," Naomi said. "The window was open and the screen too. It was practically an invitation."

"Practically," Officer Gerst agreed pleasantly as he removed a notebook from his shirt pocket and began writing in it. "The dispatcher said you reported an intruder. Did you mean an intruder other than you two, or are you both turning yourselves in?"

Liz stood. "You're spending too much time around Chief Houghton. You're starting to sound like him. Someone was hiding in the bathroom, and the person wore black clothes and a dark ski mask." She went on to tell him the details of their encounter, admitting her and Naomi's activity as well.

Officer Gerst stopped writing and looked up at them. "You two could have been hurt."

Liz felt a twinge of guilt since one of them *was* hurt a little. She noticed that Naomi hadn't stood when she did and wondered about her friend's ankle. "I know, but I wanted to find out more about Nora Wexler."

He raised his eyebrows. "The murdered woman at the courthouse?"

"The same."

"As I remember, you thought your break-in was related to her death."

"And it was," Liz said. "As Chief Houghton could tell you, the person who broke into my quarters was looking for an emerald that Nora was keeping from her ex-husband."

"The missing crystal was an emerald?" he asked.

Liz nodded.

Officer Gerst whistled. "That makes your burglary more interesting."

"Thanks," she said dryly. "I'd hate to have a boring burglary."

Again the young officer's cheeks pinked. He glanced at the house. "So, do you think your ninja might have been searching for the emerald inside?"

"Maybe," Liz said. "Obviously, Jessica Ellis and her sister knew where the gem ended up since Jessica broke into my room. But it's possible they didn't share the news with Will Wexler. If he killed Nora for the gem, he could have broken in here looking for it."

Officer Gerst tapped his notebook with the tip of his pen. "Can you tell me anything about the intruder, other than the black clothes and ski mask?"

"He wasn't very tall, assuming it was a man," Naomi answered.

Liz realized that Naomi was right. Everything had happened so quickly that she'd barely noticed, but the person couldn't have been any taller than Liz herself.

"We should find out how tall Will is," Liz said.

Officer Gerst shook his head. "What *you* should do is stay out of an open police investigation. Before I left the station, the chief told me not to arrest you two for breaking in here, but he said I should give you both a good scolding." He shrugged. "Consider yourselves scolded."

"Are you going to check inside?" Liz asked.

"Yes." He pointed at them. "You both wait out here."

"I'll go with you," Liz suggested. "I can tell you if the intruder took anything on his way out."

"You said he was running," the officer reminded her.

"When I *saw* him," Liz said, "but he knocked us down, so there was some time before we got up. He could have grabbed something then."

"The intruder assaulted you?" Officer Gerst looked each of them over. "Are you all right?"

"I'm fine," Liz said.

"Me too," Naomi chirped.

"Naomi twisted her ankle. If it's swollen when we leave, I'll drive her by the clinic."

"Don't I get a say?" Naomi asked.

Liz noticed her friend still hadn't stood up. "Maybe not. I'm not going to leave you alone at your house if you can't walk."

"It's not that bad."

"I need to check inside," Officer Gerst said. He gestured toward Liz before slipping his notebook back into his pocket. "You can come with me, but don't touch anything."

Liz followed him through the house without commentary, then took the opportunity to peek into the bathroom where the intruder had hidden. She observed that Nora owned a lot of makeup, but otherwise she didn't see anything meaningful in her toiletries.

"Do you notice anything missing?" the officer asked as they walked out of the bathroom and into the bedroom. His tone suggested he didn't expect she had.

Liz made a point of surveying the room, though she didn't anticipate seeing anything new. Then she froze. She dropped to her knees and peered under the bed, then stood and looked behind the small bedside table.

"Care to share what you're searching for?" Officer Gerst asked.

Liz straightened and faced the officer. "When we were here, I picked up a photo from the fireplace mantel. It was of Nora and another woman. I was holding it when the intruder rushed out of the bathroom, but now it's missing. I thought maybe I flung it under the bed or behind the table as I fell."

"Do you think the intruder took the photograph?"

"I don't see any other options." Liz had been sure the intruder was connected to Will, but if so, why take the photograph? Could the blurry woman have been connected to him somehow? Liz had believed it was Prudence, but what if she was wrong?

After Officer Gerst took careful notes on the missing photograph, they walked out of the apartment. He turned the lock and closed the door behind him as they left.

Naomi was standing by the porch rail. "Find anything?"

"The photo is missing," Liz said.

"The one of Nora and Prudence?"

"I thought it was Prudence, but if the intruder is Will, why would he steal a photo of Nora and Prudence?" Liz asked.

Naomi thought about it for a moment. "I don't remember the photo that well. We were mostly focused on those two people. Maybe someone else appeared in the background. Or maybe Nora was wearing something that is relevant. Did the photo show her hands? Maybe this has to do with the emerald."

Liz sighed. "I don't know. Her hands might have been showing. I mostly noted how young she looked and how much nicer she seemed than when I met her at the courthouse. I wish I'd taken more time to study the photo."

"I think we're done here," Officer Gerst said. "And since I can't leave until you two leave, may I walk you to your car?"

Liz closely watched Naomi walk, but her friend was barely limping at all. Clearly, she really had only twisted her ankle a little. "Do you want me to drive you home or back to the bakery?" she asked as they got into Liz's black sedan.

"Bakery," Naomi said. "There's still time for me to close up. I hate to leave that for the others."

"How's your ankle?" Liz asked.

"It's fine." Naomi laughed. "You know, you can be a tiny bit of a mother hen."

"I feel guilty about you getting hurt while helping me break into a murder victim's home," Liz said.

"When you put it that way, it does sound pretty awful." Naomi took in Liz's expression and laughed again. "Honestly, I'm fine. And

I loved the adventure. Plus, if you're going to have an adventure, it's more fun to have it with a friend."

Liz forced a weak smile, but she still felt guilty.

Once she dropped off Naomi, she was soon back in the inn. She walked to the sitting room to see if it needed any straightening up before the coffee hour. To her surprise, Gwen sat on one of the sofas with Brya, both busily hand sewing. At their feet, Pixie and Beans were napping with their noses touching.

Brya caught sight of Liz and hopped down from the sofa, startling the dogs and sending Pixie racing in circles around the bewildered-looking bulldog. Brya dashed across the room, carrying her work over to Liz.

"Look at what Miss Gwen taught me," she said, holding the project practically under Liz's nose. "When I finish it, I'm going to put it on my bedroom wall."

Liz blinked and drew back enough for her eyes to focus. The piece used folded fabric in different shades of green, a technique Liz had seen used to make Christmas ornaments, but the child was arranging the folded fabric like overlapping scales. "Are you making snake skin?"

Brya shook her head, sending her ponytail swinging. "They're *dragon* scales."

"Oh, they should be lovely when you're done," Liz said. She glanced at Gwen. "It was certainly nice of Mrs. Paulson to show you."

"She's really nice," Brya agreed as she returned to the couch. Beans huffed and dropped back down to lay at her feet while Pixie danced around beside him. "And she's not even mad about Cleopatra."

"Not that I want to get that close to a snake again," Gwen said. She turned to Liz. "I'm not a huge fan of scales, but since Brya apparently was fond of scaly creatures, I thought she might like this project."

"That's very perceptive of you," Liz said. "Do you have kids of your own?"

Gwen shook her head. "My husband and I were both in the military. I was an army nurse. Back then, having kids never seemed to fit into our lives." She smiled down at Brya, bent over her work studiously. "But I remember what it's like to be young, bright, and bored. It's the same thing that sent me into the military in the first place. I was looking for adventure."

"I'm so glad Brya has found something she enjoys," Liz said. "Where's her mom?"

Gwen chuckled. "Probably having a long, quiet soak or a nap. She's taking Brya back at the coffee hour."

Brya stopped working for a moment and glanced at Liz. "Are we going to have more of those lemon bars? They were yummy."

"Something even better," Liz promised. "Just wait."

To her surprise, the child didn't pout at not getting the answer she wanted. Instead, she simply agreed and continued working on the project in her lap. *Will wonders never cease? Maybe things are looking up*, Liz thought.

She excused herself and went to the kitchen to put on fresh coffee as she knew the other guests would soon be gathering in the sitting room. After she measured the rich coffee and water into the coffeemaker, the machine began to gurgle and the dark-brown liquid dripped into the coffeepot. The scent filling the room made Liz's mouth water.

On impulse, while she waited on the coffee, Liz grabbed her laptop from the counter, booted it up, and did an online search for Prudence Spratt. She frowned when the search returned only a few names, none of them in Pleasant Creek and most far too old to be the Prudence she was looking for.

She was still trying to think of a way to force the computer to give her the information she needed when the phone rang. As it was the landline, Liz knew it had to be inn business, and she snagged the phone with one hand. "Olde Mansion Inn, may I help you?"

A hoarse whisper spoke fiercely in her ear: "Mind your own business or else."

15

Hanging up the phone with a shaking hand, Liz struggled to calm down. *You'd think this was the first time I'd ever gotten a nasty phone call*, she chided herself, but her racing heart didn't seem to care. It didn't help that she was bombarded with memories of Nora's swollen face as she gasped for breath.

"Stop it," she scolded herself. She concentrated on remembering the voice. Had it been male or female? Young or old? Accented? She was fairly certain it wasn't accented, but beyond that she simply didn't know. It was hard to judge the voice because the person had whispered only a few words.

Should I call the police? Liz rested her hand on the phone, drumming her nails against the hard surface. Did she really want to chat with the police so soon after breaking into Nora's house? She feared she might be considered more of an annoyance than a help with her latest adventure. And what could they do about the call anyway?

She was so deep in thought that she nearly jumped out of her skin when the kitchen door swung open and a male voice said, "Liz?"

She spun around to see Jackson grinning at her and holding up a package wrapped in newspaper. Suddenly, she was very glad to see the handsome mayor of Pleasant Creek. She crossed the room in seconds and hugged him fiercely.

"Wow," Jackson said, chuckling as he returned the hug. "I don't know what I did to deserve that greeting, but if you'll let me know, I'll do it again."

Liz took a step back. "It's been a tough week so far, and I've missed you. Did you have a good trip and catch a lot of fish?"

"More than I know what to do with, so I brought you some." He handed over the paper-wrapped package. "They're all cleaned and beheaded, but I didn't fillet them."

"I'm just happy not to need to clean fish," Liz said, taking the package. "Thank you. I do love fresh fish." She carried the package to the fridge. "Do you want a cup of coffee?"

"Sure, I'm not back on the clock yet, and I want to hear about your challenging week. I hope there's nothing wrong with Steve."

At the mention of her godson, Liz turned to smile at Jackson from the coffeemaker, touched that he knew her so well. "No, I spoke to Steve on Sunday. He was talking about possibly getting some leave in the fall, but it's too soon to tell." Liz loved her godson like her own. She'd raised him since he was seven, after he lost his parents in a car crash. He'd grown up to be a fine young man, and she was immensely proud of him. But he was also serving overseas in Kosovo, so she worried about him.

"If it's not Steve, what made the week so bad?" Jackson asked.

"It's a long story." Liz picked up the mugs of coffee. "If none of the guests are out there, let's sit in the four-season room with the coffee, and I'll tell you all about it."

As she'd hoped, the cheerful room with its rattan furniture and tall windows was empty. She and Jackson settled on the love seat that faced the longest row of windows, giving them a view of Jaynes Lake in the distance. The sun sparkled on the water.

Jackson took a sip of his coffee, waiting patiently for Liz to begin the story. She started with her jury duty experience. He listened without speaking, though he reached out and squeezed her hand as she described Nora's allergic reaction. When she got to the break-in, his face clouded.

But the description of her breaking-and-entering adventure caused him to shift in his seat, and he finally blurted out, "You have to be more careful."

"We were fine," Liz assured him. "I'm almost done." She explained about the missing photo and ended with her nasty phone call.

"I don't like this at all," Jackson said. "Especially with you getting threats."

"It's not exactly the first time I've ever been threatened," she said. "Whoever actually killed Nora is still out there. I don't think it was Jessica or her sister, since they were at the police station with Chief Houghton when Naomi and I ran into the intruder at Nora's house."

"That's a theory we can check into right now." Jackson pulled out his phone from his pocket and dialed the police station. He identified himself and asked to speak to Chief Houghton. Within moments, he was asking the chief if Jessica and her sister were still in custody. "Yes, I'm here with Liz and hearing about all this for the first time." His serious expression softened into a smile for a moment. "Do you know of anyone who can keep Liz out of trouble when she sets her mind to it?"

Liz crossed her arms over her chest, not sure she liked being talked about. She wasn't actually interested in getting into trouble. She was interested in answers. Especially since trouble had forced itself on her at the courthouse and seemed intent on following her home. Liz had an inn to run, and she didn't see how she could keep her home safe until whoever was responsible for the murder was behind bars. Her musings made her miss Jackson's next few remarks because she was surprised when he shut off his phone.

"According to the chief, the sisters produced a lawyer nearly the second they arrived at his office. They weren't there long."

"So they could have been playing ninja at Nora's house," Liz said.

Jackson nodded. "Or it could have been Nora's ex, whom I assume is your favorite suspect."

"I don't know." Feeling jittery, Liz thought she had probably had enough coffee, so she set her half-full mug down on the glass-topped table in front of them. "I believe Jessica, I think, but that doesn't automatically mean it was Will Wexler."

"I wish you'd leave the detecting to the police." Before she could speak, he held up a hand. "You don't have to say anything. I know better than to expect it."

"I don't intend to put myself into any dangerous situations," Liz said. Then at Jackson's incredulous expression, she added, "Truly. But I'm not sure the police are questioning the right people. You know what I think would really help? If I could talk to Nora's old friend Prudence Spratt. She would have an outside view of Nora's ex and possibly of the whole Wexler family."

"So ask her."

"I can't find her," Liz said. "I did an Internet search on her name, and I tried the phone book. I also asked Miriam. She knew Nora and Prudence when they were young, but she doesn't know what happened to Prudence."

"I could possibly track down the woman," Jackson said, setting his now empty mug beside Liz's. "As the mayor, I may have access to a little more information than you. Though I'm only likely to find her if she stayed in the area. It doesn't sound like there was much to keep her here."

"I don't know," Liz said. "She tried to come back to the community once. I'm not sure it would have been easy for her to leave completely."

"You have quite a few theories about a woman you've never met," Jackson said.

"With your help, maybe we can change that last part," Liz replied. "I'm grateful for your help." Then she smiled. "And for the fish."

"You're welcome for both," Jackson said, "but I'd feel better if you'd promise to be more careful."

"I promise."

Jackson left soon after, and Liz took the package of fish out of the fridge and pulled her fillet knife out of the knife block. She'd fillet the fish, then freeze them in dinner-size portions. Then she could have some of the beautiful fish whenever she wanted. Her mouth watered at the thought, and she decided on some nice baked fish for supper.

While she was working, Sadie slipped into the kitchen. "I saw Jackson's car from the windows of Sew Welcome. I wanted to pop in and say hi, but we had a customer who had a million questions about cotton versus linen yarn."

"Wow, I'm not sure I could come up with a million questions about any kind of yarn," Liz said.

"Nitpicker," Sadie scolded as she walked over to the coffeepot and poured a cup. "That fish is gorgeous."

"Do you want some?" Liz asked. "Jackson gave me enough to last until winter."

"I notice he *cleaned* it for you," Sadie said, putting heavy emphasis on the word.

"So?"

"When a man cleans the fish before he hands it over, you know he's in love," Sadie declared.

Liz felt her cheeks warm and knew she must be blushing, but she refused to react to Sadie's teasing. "I'm sure he just had too much fish and figured I didn't know how to clean them."

"Sure he did," Sadie said wryly. "He's showing you what a good provider he is. It's instinctive in men, I tell you."

"Because you're an expert on men." Liz pointed at Sadie with the tip of her fillet knife. "You keep up the teasing, and there will be no fish for you."

Sadie boomed out a laugh. "It's hard to resist when it's so easy to *bait* you."

Liz winced. "That's terrible."

Sadie was still laughing as she carried her mug from the kitchen.

Liz finished packaging the fish, then made another fresh pot of coffee and carried the tarts out for social hour. She found her guests fussing over Pixie in the sitting room. The little dog was doing tricks for Brya and generally charming the whole group, including Beans who gazed at his new fluffy girlfriend in obvious adoration. The group was pleasant, and Liz felt herself beginning to relax for the first time all day.

Liz perched on the edge of a chair, ready to hop up if anyone needed her. She was surprised when Courtney changed seats, choosing a chair near Liz and then scooting the chair even closer. "I wanted to thank you for a wonderful stay," she said.

Liz looked at her in surprise. "Are you leaving?"

"No, but things are so hectic when it's time to go, and I didn't want to forget to tell you." Her gaze turned toward her daughter who was giggling as Pixie jumped into her lap and licked her face. "Brya has had a difficult time this year. Her nana died, and they did so many things together. She's been very sad and hard to handle. I guess this trip was my attempt to fill the void."

"It seems like it helped."

"For a while there, it wasn't looking good. I tried to spend every second with Brya, and I think I was suffocating her. Plus, she wasn't really interested in helping with my quilt project, but she's thrilled to be working on her dragon-scale wall hanging. Gwen was a godsend. I'm glad to know there are still good and kind people around."

"I guess that's part of the saying about child-rearing," Liz said. "It takes a village."

"Or sometimes just a quilting inn."

When the coffee hour was over and the guests started to scatter to make their dinner plans, Liz carried the dishes into the kitchen, feeling considerably lighter in spirit. As she came back for the last load of cups, she saw Pixie was finally tuckered out and had fallen asleep, using Beans as a pillow.

The phone in the kitchen rang, and Liz hurried out to snatch it up. Worried that it might be another harassing call, she took a deep breath before saying, "Olde Mansion Inn, may I help you?"

Liz didn't recognize the deep voice that responded, "May I speak to Liz Eckardt?"

"Speaking."

"Good evening, Miss Eckardt. I would like to meet with you to clear up some things about the death of my ex-wife."

"Mr. Wexler?"

"Obviously. Miss Eckardt, I think the police have gotten entirely the wrong idea about my family and their relationship with Nora, and I presume you've played a part in that."

Liz didn't like the accusatory tone, but she merely said, "I'm listening."

"I don't want to do this over the phone," he said. "Could you come to my home this evening?"

Liz knew that *not* racing over to the house of her own personal prime suspect at night was exactly the sort of thing Jackson was talking about when he'd asked her to be careful. Of course, if she took someone with her, then she would be showing a reasonable amount of care. "I'll be happy to speak with you, but I'm not coming alone."

"I would rather not involve the police in this discussion."

"Not a policeman," Liz said. "But I'm not in the habit of meeting strangers at night by myself."

"Bring a friend if you like," the man said. "Could you be here by seven o'clock?"

"Probably," Liz said. "Though it would be best if you gave me your number so I can call you if I need to change the time."

"That will be fine." He rattled off his address and phone number, and Liz jotted them down on the pad she kept by the phone. As soon as the call ended, she dialed Jackson's number. "I know you barely got home, but I wondered if you'd be free to meet Will with me this evening at seven."

"The ex-husband of the murdered woman?" Jackson sounded shocked. "Are you sure that's wise?"

"He called me, and this is me being careful by not going alone. Unless you can't come."

"Of course I can come," Jackson said. "Though I'm surprised you called me instead of Naomi. Isn't she usually your partner in crime?"

"I try to spread my questionable adventures around," Liz said. "And I've already dragged Naomi into some light breaking and entering. Besides, you're the one who told me to be careful."

"I did. How about I come and pick you up?"

"Sounds good." Liz hung up, hoping she'd made the right decision. It was always possible that Nora's ex-husband would be more cautious with Jackson there. Though, if Will *was* the killer, surely he would be much less likely to attack the mayor of Pleasant Creek.

She ate a light dinner of baked fish and steamed vegetables, then ran a brush through her hair before heading out to the front porch to wait on Jackson. The day's heat had already begun to dissipate, even though it wasn't dark yet, and a welcome breeze blew across her face.

As Liz watched the cars pass on the street, she missed the *clip-clop* of hooves. During the day, Amish buggies would be sprinkled into the traffic, but most Amish families were done with their chores in town before evening. She found that her phone chat with Nora's ex-husband hadn't ruffled the calm she'd gotten from the coffee hour. Of course, she hadn't actually *met* the man yet.

A vintage pickup parked in front of the inn, and Liz stood, recognizing it immediately.

Jackson got out of the truck and circled the front to hold open the passenger door. "Your chariot awaits."

Liz chuckled as she came down the steps from the porch. "My chariot is a 2014 black Acura TL sedan, with a leather interior and all the bells and whistles."

"Are you dissing my ride?" Jackson asked, his stern tone belied by the twinkle in his eyes.

"I would never, ever dis your ride," Liz said as she stepped around Jackson and climbed into the truck, "since you once saved my life with it."

She told him the address, and they were soon on their way, traversing through the slower evening traffic easily. Though the truck was meticulously maintained, it was still a pickup, and Liz could feel every bump in the road, reminding her of why she loved her own vehicle so much.

Jackson offered her a sideways glance. "So, am I just the muscle tonight? You talk and I glower?"

She grinned. "You're not all that good at glowering."

"I can glower," he protested. "I can scowl, glare, and intimidate as well."

"I'm pretty sure you can do some of those at the same time," Liz said. She glanced over at Jackson, appreciating as always his rugged good looks and the muscles he'd acquired in the furniture-building business. She could imagine him being physically intimidating, but his personality was so amicable that he was hard not to like. And Liz liked him very much.

He caught her glancing at him and smiled. "You look good."

She laughed. "I look exactly the same as when you saw me a few hours ago."

"You looked good then too," he said.

"Thank you."

They rode in friendly silence for a few miles, and Liz watched the shops pass, soaking in the charm of the little town. As they drove into more residential areas, she thought of all the people who had warned her that she'd miss Boston terribly when she moved away to the countryside. The truth was she rarely missed anything about city life. Relocating to Pleasant Creek had been like coming home.

"Penny for your thoughts?" Jackson said.

"That's an old-fashioned saying," Liz responded.

"I'm an old-fashioned guy."

"I was thinking about how much I love Pleasant Creek."

"I'm glad," Jackson said. "Though you've certainly seen the darker side of the area a time or two."

"But when it comes to people, one bad apple doesn't spoil the whole bunch. There are wonderful people here."

"I agree." He glanced in her direction again. "Thanks for taking what I said about being careful seriously. I'm glad you asked me to come along." Before she could respond, he pointed out the front window. "We're coming up on our destination."

Liz leaned forward. A pale silver Lexus was parked at the curb in front of the handsome Craftsman home. The redbrick house was clearly undergoing some repairs. Liz saw stacks of bricks next to the front porch. Another pallet of bricks blocked the end of the short driveway to the house.

"I'll let you off here, then swing around and park on the other side of the street," Jackson said. "Don't go in until I catch up with you."

Liz grinned. "Worrywart."

"Guilty as charged," he said.

Liz hopped out and walked over to the neatly laid brick walkway leading to the house. Then she waited for Jackson.

When he trotted across the street, he said, "I'll follow your lead."

"Thanks." Liz marched up to the brick porch with Jackson directly behind her. She rapped on the door.

The slightly built man who answered the door had close-cropped red hair and lightly freckled skin, and he held a pair of reading glasses. Liz noticed right away that he was almost exactly her height, meaning he could have easily been the intruder in Nora's home.

"You must be Liz Eckardt," he said, extending his hand. "Thank you for coming on such short notice."

After Liz shook his hand, Wexler's gaze traveled back to where Jackson stood. "Mayor Cross, this is a surprise. Miss Eckardt said she was bringing a friend, but I didn't expect the mayor."

Jackson stepped closer and offered his hand. "I don't believe we've met."

"We have," Wexler said, "but you probably don't remember. It was at a fund-raising event when you first ran for mayor. My mother dragged me along. Perhaps you remember her, Fiona Wexler?"

Jackson nodded. "I hope she's well."

"Rattling around in the old family home but happy about it." He stepped back and gestured into the house. "Please come in and let's be comfortable."

"I'm looking forward to what you can tell me about your ex-wife, Mr. Wexler," Liz said. "I met her only briefly before her allergic reaction."

"Please call me Will," he said as he led them into the living room.

The polished wood floors were mostly bare, with only scattered rugs, much like Liz preferred it at the inn. A small brick fireplace on one wall had a neat wooden mantel in the same dark honey tones as the floor. The room was lightly furnished, but Liz could tell every piece was an antique. She would have trouble coming up with the money it would cost to replace the furniture in that one room.

"This is a beautiful old house," Liz said.

"It was built in 1917," Will said. "It was declared a historic home years ago, which means all remodeling must go through a rather lengthy process. Sometimes the extensive rules to keep historic homes authentic make it hard to keep them repaired."

"I've heard that," Jackson said, "but I'm always glad to see history preserved."

Will invited Liz and Jackson to sit on the leather mission-style sofa. "I know your meeting with Nora wasn't pleasant. My ex-wife could be a difficult person."

"And she was keeping you from the future you wanted," Liz said, "by holding on to the emerald from your family's engagement ring."

Will gave her a tight smile. "You're well informed."

"Since this keeps intruding on my life, it seemed best that I be informed," she said. "Especially because your fiancée and her sister felt it necessary to ransack my private quarters instead of simply asking me for the emerald."

Color crept into Will's cheeks. "That was poor judgment, but this situation is very serious for my family. I suppose Rebecca feared we could end up with another person holding the emerald over our heads."

"I'm sure once the police are finished, you'll get your emerald back," Liz said. "Since Nora is dead."

Will appeared stunned by her blunt tone. "I had nothing to do with Nora's death. Neither did Rebecca or Jessica. Yes, we wanted the emerald back to ensure the inheritance would pass without a hitch to any children Rebecca and I might have, but we had a backup plan."

"One that didn't include Nora's death?" Liz asked.

"I was going to have a new emerald set in the ring." Will rubbed his forehead. "You have to understand, it's really the setting that's key. That's what is irreplaceable. And I already had it."

"Did you worry that putting a new emerald in the ring could create inheritance problems?" Liz pressed.

"Maybe. But probably not," Will responded. "Sure, I would have liked the original emerald, so there was no chance that anyone could argue we hadn't fulfilled the demands of the inheritance, but it was only a minor chance that anyone would try to contest based on that. It was a chance I preferred not to take but not one I seriously feared."

"Yet apparently your fiancée worried about it enough that she was willing to have her sister break into my rooms."

"Rebecca can be impulsive," Will said.

"Clearly." Liz sat back on the sofa. "Why did you ask me to come over? You could have said this on the phone."

"Jessica seems to think you have a special relationship with the chief of police."

Liz laughed. "If by *special*, you mean that he thought I might be the killer at first, yes. But I still don't know what I can do for you."

Will raised both hands. "I don't know. I just want all of this to go away. I want to get married, start a family, and have a peaceful life."

"That seems a reasonable thing to want," Jackson said.

Will gave him a grateful look.

"Mr. Wexler," Liz said, then seeing the man open his mouth to object, she corrected herself. "Will, do you have any theories about who might have killed Nora?"

"None. Nora could be difficult; you experienced that. But if every abrasive person in the world became a murder victim, we'd run out of cemetery space."

"So you don't know of anyone with whom she was having specific problems," Liz said. "Other than yourself."

"For obvious reasons, I didn't spend much time with Nora since the divorce, and what time we did spend together was never pleasant," Will said. "Most of our communication was through lawyers."

"I wonder if you could tell me anything about Nora's friend Prudence Spratt," Liz said.

That brought a look of surprise to his face. "I haven't thought about Prudence in years. She was Nora's Amish friend."

"An interesting way to describe her since Nora was Amish too," Liz pointed out.

"I know, but Nora never *seemed* Amish. She was always the very square peg in the round community, and I assume everyone gave a sigh of relief when she left, though they might not admit it. Prudence, on the other hand, she seemed like the real deal, very quiet, almost shy."

"She seems an odd person to be Nora's best friend."

Will harrumphed. "Nora didn't really have friends. I think Prudence was the sort of person who liked being with someone so strong. Prudence wasn't strong, or that's how it seemed to me. I think she went back to the community not long after Nora and I got married. Leastways she stopped coming around."

"Prudence did go back to the community," Liz told him, "but she didn't stay."

"That's too bad," Will said. "As far as I could tell, she was a nice person. Just easily bullied. I tried to make her feel welcome with Nora and me, but Nora started pushing Prudence away almost the moment I put the ring on Nora's finger."

"Do you think Prudence could have been angry with Nora?" Liz inquired.

The idea seemed to startle him. "I suppose, though it's hard to picture. She was mostly hurt, I think. But that was years ago. I'm sure she moved on long before now."

Liz had to admit that it did sound like a reach to consider Prudence a suspect, but she'd still like to find the woman and learn what insights she might have into Nora's life.

Though they stayed to talk awhile longer, Liz didn't learn anything else. Nora's ex had evidently moved on and didn't have much interest in whatever Nora had been into.

"By the way," Liz said as the thought came to mind, "do you know what Nora did for a living?"

Will laughed without humor. "Spent her alimony. I paid her enough to live comfortably, and I believe she was bringing in some money from renters. Other than that, I don't think Nora ever worked. If you'd asked her, I imagine she'd have said she was self-employed since that sounds better than living off what she could take from others."

With no further questions coming to mind, Liz thanked Will for his time and stood to leave.

Will jumped to his feet. "Would you speak to the police chief and tell him to ease up on my fiancée?"

"I honestly don't have any special pull with the police," Liz said.

Will turned a hopeful look toward Jackson.

The mayor patted the man on the shoulder. "Chief Houghton is very good at his job. He'll find the real killer, and then everyone can go on with their lives."

"I hope so."

When Liz and Jackson went outside, she saw that dusk had finally fallen. A single streetlamp in front of Will's house was lit, throwing a golden pool of light around it. Liz and Jackson walked through it and stepped off the curb to cross the street.

Liz turned at the sound of a motor revving. Then bright headlights blinded her as a car roared toward them. Jackson threw his arm around her waist and lurched back out of the road, towing Liz along with him.

The car raced by, missing them by inches.

Liz gasped and stared at Jackson. "Someone tried to kill us!"

16

Jackson insisted that they call the police about the near hit-and-run collision. Liz didn't know what good that would do; neither of them had gotten a good look at the car in the wash of headlights and the shock of having someone try to kill them. Jackson made the call, and Chief Houghton showed up almost faster than Liz could have driven across town. *When someone tries to kill the mayor, the response time is impressive.*

"I doubt I was the driver's target," Jackson said after they described the incident. "Liz received a threatening phone call, and then this happened. I have to assume the two were related."

The chief cocked an eyebrow at Liz. "You received a threatening phone call? I haven't seen that report yet."

"I didn't report it. It was just a vague phone call." She described the whispery voice and related the warning. "I couldn't even tell if it was a man or a woman."

"I'll still add it to the growing pile of weirdness connected to this case," Chief Houghton said. "I wish I could get a handle on all this."

"I hope you do," Jackson said, his voice unusually serious. "Soon."

When Liz finally got back to the inn, it was time to lock the doors for the night. She walked through the quiet rooms downstairs feeling uncharacteristically jumpy. At one point when Pixie crept up behind her and pushed a cold nose against Liz's bare ankle, she let out a brief shriek before looking down and seeing the little dog. "Thanks for the cardio workout," she said, scooping Pixie up and stroking her fur.

The little dog snuggled against her happily, lapping at her chin.

Since Liz wasn't eager to be all alone, she brought both Beans and Pixie into her bedroom for the night where they flopped in a pile on the floor. Liz chuckled as Beans promptly began snoring. "I'm glad you two can relax."

She walked over and peered out the window at the darkness beyond. Someone out there had tried to kill her. She thought about the meeting with Will and how odd she'd found it that he wanted her to drive to his house for something that could have been discussed over the phone easily enough. Could he have wanted her at the house so that his fiancée would have the opportunity to run her down? And how long would it be before the driver tried again?

Finally, she forced herself away from the window and got ready for bed. Her sleep was fitful, her dreams full of danger and shadows.

In the morning, Liz woke feeling stiff and fuzzy-headed. Unfortunately, her roommates for the night had slept well and begged to go outside. Pixie raced in circles around Beans, and even the bulldog whined and head-butted the bedroom door.

"Fine," Liz said. "Let me throw on some clothes, and I'll take you both for a walk."

At the word *walk*, Pixie went into a frenzy of yipping and dancing around Liz's feet, making her dressing a challenge. She managed without catastrophe and pulled her hair back into a ponytail. Since she didn't have a leash for Pixie, she removed a long shoestring from a pair of sneakers and tied it to the loop on the dog's collar. It wasn't much of a leash, but the little dog didn't have Beans's heft, so Liz was fairly sure she could hold on to it.

Liz opened the door before both dogs exploded. Once she was outside, the creeping nervousness from the night before returned in full force. As she paced around the yard, every bush looked like a great place for an attacker to lie in wait, and every car that passed made her jump. She might have given in to the nerves and rushed back inside except for the dogs, who didn't appear to be worried.

Liz gave herself a mental shake. If someone was lurking in the yard, Beans would let her know. She had more than enough proof of that from past adventures.

When Beans and Pixie had finished sniffing every bush and flower, Beans must have remembered that breakfast comes after a walk, because he started dragging Liz toward the inn with Pixie following him cheerfully. Then both dogs froze and turned toward the street.

The breath caught in Liz's throat. She turned to look, only to see a sporty little blue car pull in and park in front of the inn.

Jessica climbed out and headed straight for Liz. "Pixie, baby," the woman called. "I've missed you."

Pixie barked and tugged on the shoestring leash, finally yanking the end out of Liz's hand. Pixie raced to her mistress, trailing the shoestring behind her. Jessica picked her up and carried her back over to Liz.

Beans looked at Pixie and gave a disgruntled bark, but the little dog ignored him.

"I'm sorry to take such a long time to come back," Jessica told Liz. "I was completely frazzled after the police let me go, so I went straight home for a glass of wine and a good cry. I knew Pixie was in good hands. I hope she behaved."

"She was fine," Liz said. "The rest of the guests enjoyed her, and I think Beans may be in love."

"Oh, isn't that adorable," Jessica cooed down at the bulldog.

"I met your sister's fiancé last night," Liz stated.

"Will?" Jessica said. "He's a great guy. I'm glad he and Rebecca will be able to get on with their lives. I mean, I'm sorry that Nora died, but she wasn't a nice woman."

"Apparently not," Liz said. "Did your sister happen to go home with you after you were both done with the police?"

Jessica shook her head. "I think she was probably in a hurry to go see Will after everything that happened. Why?"

"Because my visit to see Will ended in someone trying to run me over with a car," Liz said. "And it left me wondering if the near hit-and-run accident was something set up by Will and your sister."

Jessica stared at her in shock. "Absolutely not. I'm sorry you had such a horrible experience, but my sister had nothing to do with it. Rebecca isn't like that. She would never, ever do something like that, and neither would Will. They're good people; they honestly are."

Liz studied the young woman's face. She believed Jessica. Or, at least, she believed that Jessica wasn't lying. That didn't mean she wasn't wrong. It simply meant that if Will and Rebecca had tried to kill Liz, they hadn't included Jessica in the plan. "I appreciate what you're saying," Liz said.

She wasn't sure Jessica was satisfied with her answer, but the younger woman dropped the subject. Instead, she meekly asked if she could go upstairs and get her things from the room.

"Of course," Liz said. "I have to get started on breakfast, but if you don't mind coming to the kitchen, we can settle your bill after you pack."

"I'll find you," Jessica said.

As Liz beat eggs for breakfast, the conversation with Jessica swirled around in her head, along with all the events of the last few days. She felt like she was trying to work a jigsaw puzzle with a picture that kept changing. Before her enemy tried to attack her again, Liz *needed* to learn more about Nora, so she could get a better sense of where her antagonist might be.

Jessica didn't finish packing until after Liz had served breakfast, so Liz invited her to join them. The young woman seemed touched by the invitation and took a seat at the table between Gwen and Davidia. At first, the conversation was awkward and the guests kept giving Jessica curious glances. They could tell something was going on, but as Liz hadn't shared details, they didn't know what it was.

Later, after Jessica left, Liz was sweeping the foyer, and she noticed

Beans sitting near the front door, gazing mournfully at it. "Missing your girlfriend?" she asked him as she stopped to scratch his ears.

He rolled his eyes toward her, but he didn't break into tail wagging as he normally would.

"Maybe she'll come visit sometime. Or you can go see her." *Assuming her human auntie isn't a killer.*

After as much cleaning as she could stand, Liz was practically jumping out of her skin. She needed to *do* something, investigate, find more information, *anything.* Impulsively, she decided to go over to the courthouse. After all, it was where Nora was attacked. And afterward, she could stop and visit Jackson to see if he'd dug up anything on Nora's Amish friend.

When walking to her car, she was grateful for her choice of a light silk T-shirt and billowy pants as the weather had gotten much hotter since her morning dog walk. She'd considered walking to the courthouse to avoid the struggle of finding a parking space, but the heat quickly dissuaded her, and she certainly enjoyed the air-conditioning in her car on the drive over. She had to circle the parking lot three times before a space opened up at the far end. "Guess I'll get in some walking time after all," she muttered as she slipped into the space.

She passed through security easily, then noticed that she recognized one of the two security guards. "You were here on the day the woman had the allergic reaction."

The guard's professional smile slipped away. "It was awful. And the poor woman died."

"But you and the other security guard definitely did what you could. I guess everyone did."

"My niece is allergic to peanuts," the guard said. "I saw her have a mild attack once, but the meds worked for her. Now I'm twice as scared for her." She shuddered slightly. "Who would think that something as little as a beesting could do that to someone?"

"It is horrifying," Liz said. "Did you see anything weird that day?"

The guard's forehead wrinkled. "Weird? You mean, weirder than someone wheezing and swelling up like a tick?"

"I meant from other people," Liz clarified. "Did you see anyone acting oddly?"

The woman shook her head. "My attention was on that poor woman."

Liz thanked her for her time and headed for the elevator. When she got up to the fourth floor where the jury waiting room was located, she walked quietly down the hall and peeked into the room. No one was inside. Liz entered the waiting room, letting her memories of that day come back as she glanced around. She tried to picture the other people in the room, especially the ones seated near Nora. None jumped out in her memory.

"May I help you?" The jury clerk stood in the doorway, looking at her quizzically.

"Hi. I was here for jury duty on the day Nora Wexler died from the beesting," Liz explained. "It was such an upsetting day, and I've been trying to understand it. I thought maybe coming here would help me sort out my feelings about it."

The woman stared in response for a moment, then nodded. "It was pretty awful. I'd never seen anything like it." She cringed at the memory.

Liz walked closer to her and noticed the clerk was pale, with dark circles under her eyes. "Have you been ill?" she asked gently.

The clerk lay a hand on her cheek. "I think I'm coming down with something. There's nothing worse than summer flu."

"Do you have a minute to talk to me about that day?" Liz asked.

The woman took a step back. "I don't know. I'm terribly busy."

"The reason I ask is that things have been very strange since that day," Liz said urgently, "and last night I was almost killed."

The clerk's eyes widened. "Come back to my office." She spun around and practically ran. Once they were inside the small office, the clerk shut the door. She motioned for Liz to sit, and then the clerk took the chair behind the old, metal desk.

The clerk sat silently for a moment before blurting out, "I think someone is trying to kill me."

17

The shock of hearing that someone else connected with Nora's death was afraid for her life shook Liz deeply. "Have you told the police?" she asked.

The clerk shook her head in a short, jerky movement. "They look like accidents, but no one is that accident-prone, not even me." She looked intently at Liz. "Did yours look like an accident?"

"Someone tried to run me over with their car," Liz replied, then held up her hand. "We should start at the beginning, but before we do, I want to introduce myself. I'm Liz Eckardt."

The clerk nodded. "I remember you."

Liz doubted it because the woman had barely even glanced at her when she'd signed her in, but she certainly didn't want to argue with the first big clue she'd gotten so far.

The clerk straightened up in her chair and offered her hand across the desk. "I'm Sue Thompson."

The woman had complained of possibly coming down with the flu, so Liz hesitated a moment, staring at her hand.

Sue noticed and smiled slightly. "I'm not really getting the flu. I'm simply troubled by the accidents, and I can't sleep."

"Oh." Liz shook her hand. "It must be horrible for you."

"How are *you* sleeping?"

"After almost getting run over last night, not so great. What kinds of accidents have you had?"

"There have been three. I regularly take the stairs here instead of the elevator because I can use the exercise. I spend most of my day sitting in a chair," Sue said. "Anyway, when I reached the top step right on this floor, it was slick. I fell down the stairs. I was only banged up, but they're concrete stairs. It could have been much worse."

Liz offered her a sympathetic smile. "I'm sure falling down the stairs was painful and frightening. Do you know what was on the step?"

"I'm not sure. It was something oily. I told security, and they decided someone must have spilled salad dressing. How would someone in a courthouse spill a pool of salad dressing on the stairs?"

"That does seem unlikely."

"I might have ignored it," Sue continued, "if it weren't for my desk lamp. Somehow the insulation was stripped off the wires, which could touch this desk. I could have been electrocuted."

Liz looked pointedly at the desk where there was no lamp. "Do you have the lamp?"

"Not anymore. I reported it to maintenance, and they removed it. I haven't gotten a new one yet. They insisted it was ordinary wear." She frowned. "But I would have noticed. I'm very particular about my office."

Liz had to admit the office reflected that. It was clean to the point of being spartan. "You said there were three incidents?"

"I walk home after work," Sue responded. "I don't live far, and this time of year it's still light when I leave. I've never given it any thought. Pleasant Creek is such a safe town. But the night after the lamp incident, a branch from one of the trees that overhangs the sidewalk fell right as I was walking under it. I managed to dodge it, but that's when I couldn't pretend anymore. That is simply too many coincidences. But why would someone target me? I'm a widow. I live a private life."

"I don't know," Liz said.

"Could it be the same person that's after you? Maybe it's the person who killed that woman in the elevator. The police came and asked us all questions about it. I know she didn't die naturally." Sue winced. "Though nothing about the way she looked seemed natural to me."

"Allergies are natural enough," Liz said, "but it appears someone induced Nora's attack on purpose."

"Why would anyone do something like that?"

"I'm not sure. Apparently, Nora wasn't a very nice person."

Sue nodded. "I got complaints about her that day. An old man complained about her talking, but I can't *make* people be quiet. She wasn't shouting. I came in to see. Then a woman complained about some of the things she said, evidently some kind of religious bigotry. I didn't hear the words."

"Nora had a problem with the Amish," Liz said.

The clerk looked surprised. "Who could have a problem with the Amish? I don't get any of the Amish in here for jury duty, of course, because they're excused on religious grounds. But I've seen them around town. They're so quiet and polite. It seems like a peaceful way to live."

"It's difficult to understand what goes on in another person's head," Liz said, not wanting to get into Nora's life story. "I know the police are working very hard on Nora's murder investigation, but for your own safety maybe you should think about staying with friends or family until the killer is caught. And I recommend that you consider telling Chief Houghton what you've told me."

"I'd hate for him to think I'm a hysterical female," Sue said. "I think that's what the security guard thought after the salad-dressing incident."

"Chief Houghton wouldn't think that," Liz said. At least she hoped he wouldn't. "He knows someone tried to run me over last night. He'll take you seriously. I can speak to him on your behalf, but he'll want to question you as well."

Sue was quiet for a moment, then whispered, "Why?"

Liz wasn't sure what the question meant.

The clerk swallowed and continued speaking, her voice stronger. "Why would someone target us? I hardly even spoke to the victim." Then her eyes widened. "Maybe it was because you and I were both there when she was having the attack. Maybe the killer thinks the woman told us something or said something in front of us. Like a clue."

"Did you hear Nora say anything?" Liz asked.

"You mean other than accusing you of killing her?"

Liz flinched. "Nora was pretty far gone by then. She might not have been seeing clearly. She might even have been hallucinating. I know you can have hallucinations from not getting enough oxygen."

"But she still said it," Sue persisted. "And the victim had more contact with you than me. You were in the jury room with her. It makes sense to target *you*. I don't know why someone is picking on me."

Liz started feeling much less sympathetic toward the clerk. "There are many things about this case that don't make sense, but the police will sort them out. I still recommend you talk to the chief."

"I don't know." Sue glanced at the door nervously. "What if the killer is watching me? If I contact the chief, it might look like I *do* know something. Maybe you're right, and I should go stay with my cousin in Indianapolis. But for how long? Do you think the police are close to finding the killer?"

"I don't know all the details of the investigation," Liz said, "but I know they have a suspect." *Whether it was the right suspect or not.*

"That's good, so it might not be too long." Sue gave her a watery smile. "I really appreciate it that you talked to me today. On one hand, I'm terrified now that I know I'm not imagining all this, but on the other . . . it's nice not to feel so alone."

Liz reached out and patted the other woman's hand. "The police will work it out." She thanked the clerk for talking to her and left the office.

In the elevator ride downstairs, Liz contemplated her next move. She considered going by the police department to tell Chief Houghton about the mysterious accidents happening to the jury clerk. Although it sounded like none of the evidence connected to the accidents was still around, it might be possible for him to learn something from investigating.

It seems the killer has easy access to the courthouse. Then her thoughts flashed to Will's lawyer. Naturally, an attorney would have easy access to the courthouse, and no one would think twice about seeing a lawyer on the stairs or possibly even in the clerk's office.

When the elevator reached the first floor, Liz stopped at the security checkpoint again. "Hi, we talked before about the woman who died. Can I ask you one more question?"

The woman's expression turned guarded. "I suppose."

"Have you had any unusual accidents happen around you since then?" Liz asked. Logically, the guard had been as close to Nora as Liz or Sue and for even longer.

"Accidents?" The guard thought about it for a moment. "I dropped my kid's school art project on my bare foot. Those lumpy clay pots are heavier than you'd think."

"That's all?"

"That's enough," the guard said. "Every day since then my son has complained about the crack in the top of the pot."

Liz thanked her again and walked out of the courthouse. She wondered why someone would feel threatened by her and the jury clerk but not by the security guard who had dealt with the sick woman. Unless the person was targeting people who saw Nora in the jury waiting room, not people who saw her afterward. If Chief Houghton had a list of the jurors from that day, maybe he could find out if anyone else was having weird accidents.

While she was thinking, she realized she'd drifted to a grassy area to the side of the courthouse. Garden beds were planted along the sides of the space, and two marble benches offered places to sit and enjoy the flowers. Liz took advantage of one of the benches while she pondered the strange happenings.

She watched bees bustling from flower to flower in the patches of marigolds, impatiens, and petunias. Could this be where the killer had gathered the bees? There were plenty of them, drawn to the brightly colored flowers.

A warm, deep voice interrupted her thoughts. "Liz, what a lovely surprise. How are you today? I hated parting ways last night when you were still so upset."

Liz looked up into Jackson's hazel eyes. "I'm fine, honestly. I was planning to come visit you today."

"I'm always glad to hear that." He took a seat beside her on the bench.

"How are you?" Liz asked. "After all, you came as close to being run over as I did."

"I won't lie to you. I was terrified last night." The corner of his mouth turned up. "It was easier for me though. I had you to worry about. It took my mind off the near-death experience for me."

"As long as the experiences don't get any nearer to death," she responded.

A bee buzzed around the bench, circling them before flying back over to the flower bed. Liz watched it, thinking about how different the experience of being this close to bees would have been for someone with a deadly allergy. According to Miriam, Nora's mother had made Nora stay indoors. So had she continued that behavior, hiding from the creatures who could trigger such a horrible reaction? Or had she flouted the fear and sat outside to look at the flowers? Liz wasn't sure which choice she'd make, but she hoped it would be the brave one.

She jumped a little when Jackson's hand touched hers.

"You're deep in thought," he said.

"Thinking about bees."

"You're not going to let this go and allow Chief Houghton to handle it, are you?"

Liz shrugged slightly, then turned on the bench to better face him. "So, what brought you to the courthouse today?"

"I had to sign some papers."

"Have you found out anything on Prudence Spratt?" Liz asked.

Jackson laughed. "Not yet. I'm the mayor, but I'm not magic. I did ask my summer intern to look into where she might be."

"I didn't know you had an intern." Liz couldn't keep the surprise out of her voice.

He grinned sheepishly. "I don't really need one, but Scott was desperate for an internship to put on his college applications, and he's way better with the computer than me. If there's anything on Prudence, I believe he'll find it."

"I appreciate it."

They sat quietly together for a moment, gazing at the flowers.

Liz broke the silence. "Do you think this is where the killer got the bees?"

"Maybe. Though there are plenty of bees in Pleasant Creek with all the farms and gardens. It's a very green area."

Liz knew Jackson was right, but somehow she felt sure this was where the bees had originated. If the killing was planned well ahead of the day, surely the killer could have come up with a clean container that wouldn't have coated the bees with a drug residue.

She looked sideways at Jackson. "I wonder if Chief Houghton checked out the people who have a prescription for the medication that was on the bees."

"That medication for depression isn't particularly rare, so I imagine many people, even in Pleasant Creek, take it."

"Still, the chief could cross-reference people who had a prescription with people who knew Nora."

"He could," Jackson agreed, "but it seems like he believes the emerald is a much more direct clue. Wexler and his fiancée have a pretty strong motive. Nora was making them miserable."

Liz turned her gaze to the bees. "I wonder if Will or Rebecca takes that medication."

"Or his mother or his housekeeper or maybe Rebecca simply found an empty pill bottle in the trash somewhere," Jackson said. "I know it's scary for you, with the near accident last night, but I do think Chief Houghton will figure it all out."

Liz rose. "I should get back to the inn."

Jackson stood up quickly. He smiled and picked a leaf from her hair. "I could walk with you."

"I appreciate that, but I drove. I know it's not that far and I should be more ecological, but I didn't want to arrive sweaty. I could give you a lift."

"Thanks but I have errands to run while I'm out." He took her hand again, giving it a light squeeze. "I promise to bug my intern constantly until he digs up something about Prudence."

"Thank you."

It wasn't hard to sense Jackson's hesitancy to leave her, but after he made a few more stalling remarks, he turned and strode away with clear purpose.

Liz watched him go, admiring the way his broad shoulders filled out his white shirt. She had to admit that she was growing very fond of Pleasant Creek's mayor.

With a sigh, she turned toward the parking lot, trying to emulate Jackson's purposeful stride. She had plenty to do at the inn, so she promised herself that she'd only make a quick stop at the police station to tell Chief Houghton about the court clerk and ask him about checking out other people in the jury room that day.

She felt a twinge of guilt. Sarah would be busy at the inn cleaning like the wonder she was, and Liz felt she should be helping. Not that Sarah would show any sign of resentment at having an entire inn to clean. As far as Liz could tell, resentment wasn't in Sarah's emotional vocabulary. When she'd first met the young woman, Liz had wondered if that serenity in the face of hard work was true to all Amish people because Miriam had it as well. But it was clear that Nora hadn't. She'd positively oozed resentment that day in the jury waiting room.

Though she'd been only pleasantly warm while sitting on the bench among the flowers, Liz immediately felt the summer heat worsen when she crossed the paved parking lot. It seemed to shimmer off the vehicles around her as she made her way between them, and she slowed her steps in an attempt to avoid getting sweaty before she reached her car.

As she walked, she let her thoughts slip back to her conversation with Sue, again wondering why someone would target both Liz and the jury clerk. *I should have told Jackson about it. Maybe he could've made something of it.* As far as she was concerned, it virtually proved that Will's fiancée wasn't the killer. Rebecca wouldn't have even known that the clerk was close to Nora after the attack since all the prospective jurors were long gone by then.

Stepping up to the side of her car, Liz debated calling Chief Houghton instead of stopping at the station. Then she'd be sharing what she knew in the most efficient way, and it would be up to the chief if he wanted to see her.

Liz got out her keys and tried to unlock the door. She frowned. The key didn't seem to want to slip into the lock. Her attention sharpened on the car, and she groaned. The car was the same color and general shape as hers, but it definitely wasn't hers. The fuzzy dice hanging on the rearview mirror should have been a giveaway.

She wrenched the key out of the lock, annoyance with herself making her movement jerky. One of the teeth on the key caught the edge of the lock as it came out, and Liz fumbled with the rest of her keys. They hit the pavement with a jangle, and she bent down to pick them up.

Glass shattered above her head, and Liz dived for the ground. She twisted to look at the exploded window. No, not exploded. It had been struck by a bullet.

Someone was shooting at her!

18

Liz duckwalked toward the back of the car, hoping the narrow space between the two parked cars would block the shooter from seeing her. Crouching near the rear tire, she pulled out her phone with shaky hands and called the police.

When Chief Houghton arrived, he found her still crouched between the cars. "I expect the shooter is long gone," he said, reaching down to help her up.

Liz nearly burst into tears. She'd had some challenging moments since moving to Pleasant Creek, but the events of the last few days were beginning to wear her down.

The chief gave her a sympathetic look but refrained from saying anything until she'd gotten herself under control. He walked slowly around the car, then reached through the broken window to unlock the door and let himself in. He immediately found the bullet hole in the driver's seat. "I'll need to dig the bullet out before I can let you have your car back."

"It's not my car." Liz pointed farther down the row. "That's my car. I was so deep in thought, I walked to the wrong car. That's why the key didn't fit the lock right and why I dropped it. If I hadn't dropped my keys . . ." She shuddered, staring at the broken glass in the driver's seat.

"Obviously, someone thinks you know something about Ms. Wexler's murder," the chief said.

"I don't know anything that I haven't told you," she said.

"Well this doesn't make a lick of sense." He gestured to the glass. "I agree."

"I'd better find out which one of my suspects owns a gun."

Liz wasn't sure how much good that would ultimately do. Criminals weren't known to use legally obtained guns when they committed crimes much of the time. But at least it was one avenue to explore. "I'm not the only person the killer is after," Liz announced.

"Oh?"

"I talked to the jury clerk while I was inside the courthouse. I thought maybe she'd noticed something that I hadn't on the day of the murder."

Chief Houghton huffed. "Like I told you before, the clerk doesn't seem to be the noticing type. Otherwise, Rebecca Ellis wouldn't have snuck into the jury room so easily."

"That's what I thought, but someone must *think* the clerk noticed something. She's having the same kind of dangerous 'accidents' that I am, though no one has shot at her yet."

"Why is this the first time I'm hearing about it?" the chief demanded.

"The clerk wasn't sure anyone would believe her because the security at the courthouse apparently treated the events like simple accidents." Liz went on to describe the things Sue had told her.

"Yeah, I probably wouldn't pay something like that much attention if it weren't for what you've been experiencing," the chief admitted. "I'll talk to the clerk."

"She doesn't seem to know anything about Nora." Liz rubbed her arms, feeling oddly chilly despite the scorching heat. "I also talked to one of the guards who had tried to help Nora. Nothing strange has happened to her, so the killer isn't targeting everyone who was around Nora when she died. I wonder if any of the other jurors have had any suspicious accidents."

"That sounds like a long shot," Chief Houghton said, "but I'll look into it."

Liz stayed in the parking lot while the police examined the car and tracked down the owner, who raced from the courthouse to moan over the damage, making Liz feel horribly guilty when she regarded her own undamaged vehicle. When her hands stopped shaking, she asked the chief to keep her informed, then returned to the inn.

Most of the guests were out taking advantage of the clear skies and the list of activities around Pleasant Creek that Liz gave each person upon checking in.

Liz found Sarah zipping around the Amish Room with a dust mop. She admired the tidy room. "You always do such a wonderful job."

Sarah smiled shyly at her. "The room was already very clean. There wasn't much to do."

Liz wasn't surprised. Gwen struck her as the sort of person who would be insulted to find an item out of place in her home and would carry that attitude around with her to the places she stayed. "Jessica picked up her things this morning. Have you cleaned her room?"

"Not yet." Sarah looked concerned. "I did not know she had returned for her things. I will go up as soon as I finish this floor. I am almost done."

"No need," Liz said. "I could use a little cleaning to clear my head."

The Sunset Room appeared fairly neat when Liz carried the cleaning supplies and a set of fresh sheets upstairs. She started with the bathroom and soon lost herself in pine-scented productivity. Each time nerves about the shooting tried to creep back in, Liz responded with a particularly vigorous scrubbing. When she finished the bathroom, it shone as brightly as if Sarah had done it. Liz was actually rather proud of her work.

She headed into the bedroom with a duster and cleaned all the surfaces, including the tops of the windows that looked out toward the lake. She paused to admire the way the sun turned the surface of the water to diamonds. The quiet beauty of the scene and her brisk activity had begun to loosen the tension knots in her back and neck. She turned back to the room to finish dusting, polishing, and changing the bed.

Finally, she stood in the doorway with the pile of used sheets at her feet and surveyed the room. The simple contemporary decor fairly glowed from the buffing Liz had given all the light furniture. The brightly colored quilt hung perfectly straight, enlivened still more by cheery pillows. The colors of the homey rag rugs that accented the polished wood floor were only slightly more muted, and the rugs looked as though they would be inviting on bare feet.

The room didn't need anything else right now. When the next guest booked the room, they would add a bouquet of whatever might be blooming in the garden, tucked into the simple white pitcher on the dresser. Liz had already thrown away the wilted dahlias that Kiera had brought up after Jessica checked in.

It would be a lie to say she was relaxed, but Liz definitely felt more in control than she had a couple of hours ago. She gathered the bundle of dirty sheets under one arm, picked up the cleaning supply tote, and closed the door.

She found Sarah downstairs, loading the rest of the dirty sheets into a big basket in the utility room for Liz to wash.

"I don't suppose you left me any cleaning on the second floor?" Liz asked.

"No. I finished, but I have not dusted the library." Sarah gave Liz an apologetic look. "Isaac will be picking me up soon, but if you want me to dust, I can ask him to wait."

"I think you've done more than enough," Liz said. "I'll put these sheets in the washer and then tackle the library. Thank you for everything you do."

Sarah ducked her head, still shy when complimented. "I enjoy the work."

Later while Liz was in the library running a duster over the tops and edges of the books, she heard voices coming closer. She turned to see Courtney and Brya.

They both smiled brightly when they spotted Liz.

"I took Brya out to the dairy farm in your brochure," Courtney said.

"I met Lula," Brya said. "She's a cow."

"Did they tell you she sometimes leads parades here?" Liz asked.

Brya giggled. "That would be funny." She dropped her voice and whispered, "What do they do if she poops?"

Liz whispered back, "They clean it up."

For some reason, that answer brought on a fit of giggles from the little girl.

Liz was glad to see that the sullen, difficult child seemed to have disappeared in favor of this much more agreeable version.

"I cannot tell you how much we've enjoyed our stay," Courtney said. "We'll be sad when we check out tomorrow."

Brya squeaked in dismay. "Oh, I don't want to go yet. Can we stay one more day, please? I'm not done with my dragon scales, and Miss Gwen said she'd help with the finishing part."

Courtney glanced from her daughter to Liz. "Miss Eckardt might have the room booked. She may need us to make way for the next guest."

"I don't have a reservation for that room until next week," Liz assured her. "So if you're able to stay, you're certainly welcome." Then she smiled at Brya. "Assuming nothing untoward ends up in the toilets."

"I promise. Did you know Miss Gwen is a hero?" Brya boasted. "She helped soldiers when they were hurt, and she says heroes do good things. I'm going to be like that too."

"I'm glad to hear it," Liz told her, "and I hope you'll stay on to finish your project."

Brya jumped up and down, her face aglow with excitement. "Can we stay, Mom? I'll work super hard to finish."

"Then we'll stay."

Liz left the happy child and her mother, thinking about the pleasant change in Brya. *I hope it lasts.* If it does, Courtney should give Gwen a medal.

She walked on to the kitchen, a surly growl from her stomach reminding her that she hadn't had any lunch. From the fridge, she pulled some deli meat, cheese, and fresh greens from the small herb garden outside to make a sandwich. But before she could open the loaf of bread, she heard a burst of barking from the four-season room where Beans had been sulking over his missing girlfriend.

With a sigh, Liz left the sandwich makings on the counter and went to see what had upset the bulldog. She found him growling and barking at one of the windows. "What has you in such an uproar?"

Beans didn't look at her. Instead, he continued growling and barking.

Something outside had definitely upset the dog. Liz had a sudden image of the glass shattering in the parking lot and wondered if someone was lurking outside, waiting for another shot at her.

"Come on, Beans," Liz said. "Let's get away from all these windows."

The dog didn't even turn. Liz called to him repeatedly, but he kept up the barking. She crossed the room, staying as low as she could, and tried to drag the dog out of the room, but despite his short stature, he was a handful when he didn't want to go.

"Come on," she said as she tugged him inch by inch. She had him barely halfway across the room when Mary Ann and Sadie walked in.

"What's making Beans bark so much?" Sadie asked. "We could hear him from the shop."

"I don't know," Liz said, "but I think we need to get out of this room."

Sadie didn't ask any more questions. She simply marched across the room and scooped up the barking bulldog as if he were no bigger than Pixie. Then she turned to head for the door.

"Thank goodness," Liz said, standing to follow them.

Then one of the tall windows shattered, and something thumped hard against the floor.

19

Liz, Mary Ann, and Sadie screamed and stampeded out of the room. They huddled in the kitchen, staring at the doorway and waiting for the sound of more breaking glass, but the room stayed quiet.

"What was that?" Sadie asked, hugging Beans tightly against her chest.

Liz cringed. "I think someone just shot at me for the second time today."

"What?" Mary Ann and Sadie hollered in unison.

"When were you going to tell us that?" Mary Ann pressed.

"I'll tell you all about it," Liz promised. "But one attempted murder at a time."

Since the four-season room remained quiet, Liz tiptoed to the doorway and peeked around. That was when she spotted a brick on the floor. "It wasn't a gun," she called back to Sadie and Mary Ann. "Someone pitched a brick through the window."

"My goodness," Mary Ann said. "Who would do something like that?"

Liz looked over at Beans in Sadie's arms. He resembled a beanbag in dog shape and seemed content to be held. "Put Beans down," she said. "See if he thinks anyone is still outside."

Sadie dumped Beans on the floor next to the door.

The dog gave Sadie a disgruntled glance, then padded into the four-season room to snuffle the brick with little concern.

"I think it's safe," Liz said. Then she had a thought and felt like smacking herself on the head for not thinking of it before. "We should get Beans out of the room, so he doesn't end up with glass in his paws from the broken window."

Sadie scooped up the dog again. "I'll take him out to his favorite rug. You should call the police."

"I will." Liz stood over the brick, gazing down at it.

"You shouldn't pick it up," Mary Ann advised. "The police may want to check it for fingerprints."

Liz nudged the brick with the toe of her shoe. It was an old brick with crumbled corners and bits of mortar still clinging to it. She thought of the last place she'd seen piles of brick. Would the police be able to check the brick for a match to Will's house? She nudged the brick once more, this time turning it over.

On the side of the brick now facing up, someone had scrawled with a marker: *Leave it alone!*

"Leave what alone?" Mary Ann asked.

"The Nora Wexler investigation, I assume," Liz said. She pulled the phone from her pocket and called the police, thinking once again that normal people didn't spend nearly as much time on the phone with the police station.

"We should get out of here and wait for the police," Liz said after she hung up, but she stayed where she was, feeling suddenly overwhelmed by everything. She glanced at the shattered window and sighed.

"I know someone who can come and put in a new window right away," Mary Ann said, catching Liz's arm and giving her a tug. "I'll make the call from the kitchen. You'll want to close the door to this room, or you're going to have a houseful of bees." She pointed at the flowering bushes just outside where the honeybees were busy, clearly uninfluenced by the drama that had taken place over their heads.

They'd barely sat down in the kitchen before they heard a knock, this time on the side door off the utility room. Liz was surprised to see Officer Gerst standing on the step. She thought she'd graduated to Chief Houghton for all attacks and said as much.

"The chief is tied up," Officer Gerst said, then gave her a teasing grin. "Apparently, there was a commotion at the courthouse earlier today."

"I thought he'd be long done with that."

"He had more interviews connected to the case," the officer said. "You want to show me the brick? I assume you haven't handled it."

"It's untouched. You should tell Chief Houghton that Will Wexler lives in a brick house and is doing some renovations. He might want to check for a match."

"You want me to tell Chief Houghton how to do his job?" Officer Gerst asked. "I think I'll stick with letting him know what you've noticed." After he took some photos of the damage, he put on gloves, then picked up the brick and examined it.

Liz pointed toward a thick crack that ran through the brick. "Whoever did this didn't simply go to the hardware store and buy a brick. You can tell this is old."

Officer Gerst grinned at her. "The local hardware store doesn't sell bricks." Before Liz could comment, he held up a hand. "I take your meaning. Yes, this isn't a new brick. So, if it's part of the renovation at Mr. Wexler's house, it's one of the bricks being removed, not the ones being added."

Liz nodded.

Officer Gerst gazed toward the broken window. "I'll go out and check for footprints or anything else the perpetrator might have left behind. You should keep the door to this room closed."

"I will after I clean up the glass," Liz replied. "I don't want anyone getting cut."

"That's fine." He gave Liz a serious look. "It seems that someone is trying to scare you or harm you—or both. You be careful, okay?"

Liz smiled. "I'm hearing that quite often lately. I'll be as careful as I can."

As soon as Officer Gerst left, Liz set about cleaning up the broken glass, both from the floor and the window frame. While she worked, a honeybee flew around her head. She waved a hand at it, and it buzzed back out the open window.

At the sound of the door opening, Liz turned to tell whichever guest it was that the room was closed.

But instead Mary Ann stepped into the room, appearing distressed.

"What's wrong?"

"My friend is busy, so he can't get out to replace the window until tomorrow morning."

"That's all right. I'll put a sign on the door."

The rest of the day passed quietly with no new check-ins. Liz made spice cookies for the coffee hour because her recipe used honey and seemed appropriate somehow. Since most of the guests were nearing the ends of their stay, they brought their projects down to the sitting room to share techniques and work together. It made for a welcome island of tranquility in Liz's day.

When Liz went to bed, she had trouble getting to sleep with the events of the day still spinning in her head. She realized she felt completely certain that Will had killed his ex-wife and was the author of the threats against Liz, though obviously with assistance since there was no way he could have gotten outside and into a car in time to try to run over her and Jackson in the dark. Or, at least, she didn't think he could have.

If Will had planned it all along, would he have had time to sprint out a back door and into a conveniently parked car? She ran the evening over and over in her mind, finally admitting that she wasn't sure, which left her sleepless.

Several times, Liz heard Beans out in the breakfast nook, barking at the closed door to the four-season room. Each time, she walked out to see what had caught the bulldog's attention, but he never seemed really worked up, only disgruntled at not being able to get into the room. After three trips to the kitchen, Liz lugged Beans back to her quarters for the night, figuring that his snoring had to be quieter than his barking. With the rumble of bulldog snores in her ear, she drifted off well after midnight.

The next morning at breakfast, Brya poked Liz on the arm. "When will you unlock the back room with all the windows? I'd really like to go in there."

"It should be open later this morning," Liz said. "After the broken window is replaced."

Brya looked at Liz intently. "Did that sneaky ninja break the window?"

Liz set down her fork. "The ninja?"

"Yup. I saw a ninja outside last night when I looked out the window."

"When were you looking out the window?" Courtney asked her daughter.

"While you were sleeping," Brya said. "I like to look out windows when everyone is sleeping. Sometimes I see bats. Did you know a bat can eat up to twelve hundred mosquitoes in an hour?"

"My heroes," Davidia chimed in. "People don't appreciate the role that some animals play in the ecosystem. Like snakes."

"I agree," Liz said, "but I would like to know a little more about the ninja."

Davidia leaned closer to Liz. "You do realize she probably imagined that part. I mean, honestly, a ninja?"

"I did not imagine it," Brya said, a frown drawing her brows together. "And I can prove it. I took the ninja's picture."

"You took a picture in the middle of the night?" Davidia said. "I'm sure that only looks like darkness."

Brya gave her a withering look. "Hold on a second," she said. Then she jumped up from her chair and raced out of the room with her mother calling after her to walk.

Courtney turned an apologetic look toward Liz. "Brya does have a lot of imagination, but she is trying very hard to be good."

"I'm not sure she imagined it," Liz admitted. "I saw someone recently who dressed all in black with a dark ski mask. That would look like a ninja to a little girl." And it would mean that the same person who was in Nora's apartment was definitely also the one who hurled the brick through the window at the inn.

"You saw someone like that outside the inn?" Harriet asked. "Are we all safe here?"

"It wasn't here, and I'm sure we're safe," Liz said, though she wished her voice had sounded more confident. She was glad when she was saved from further questions by Brya stampeding back into the dining room.

The little girl clutched a bright pink backpack. "I keep all my investigator's gear in here," she explained.

"Investigator's gear?" Liz asked.

"Brya is very scientifically curious," Courtney said proudly. "I think a career in forensic science might be in her future."

Brya pulled a fancy camera out of the backpack and quickly called up one of the photos from its memory. Even on the small screen of the camera, the green-tinted image showed someone hiding in the bushes outside the inn. The image was shot from above, and Liz could see no way to identify the lurking figure.

Gwen looked at the picture, then up at Courtney. "That's a nice camera."

"Brya insisted on getting one after watching a show on television about Bigfoot." Courtney smiled. "She photographs every cat and raccoon that passes through our yard at night."

Brya nodded. "But the ninja is way cooler. We never have a ninja in *our* yard."

"Brya, could I borrow your camera to show the ninja picture to a policeman friend of mine?" Liz asked.

"You don't need the camera," Brya said. "I can send the picture to your cell phone."

After breakfast, Liz had time to examine the photo at length, but no details jumped out at her. Still, it was evidence, so she sent the photo to Chief Houghton's cell phone, along with a quick text explaining it. Then she slipped the phone into her pocket and braced herself for a new day.

20

Later that morning, Liz was polishing the stair rails when she noticed Harriet struggling down the stairs with her suitcases. Liz rushed up to help the older woman. "I nearly forgot you were leaving us today."

"I wish I weren't," Harriet said. "I hate leaving you here. I had another dream last night."

Liz stifled a groan, both from the older woman's words and the surprising weight of the suitcase. "I think I'll be okay. I still haven't been menaced by any green-eyed dogs or crushed under any stones."

"But you did find an emerald," Harriet said insistently. "Which is green. And it created problems for you, right? That nice girl from the third floor broke into your rooms."

"How did you know that?" Liz asked.

Harriet rolled her eyes. "Everyone knows that. Nothing remains a secret when you have a child around."

It probably depends on the child, Liz thought as they reached the first floor. She wondered what could possibly be in the heavy suitcase.

"I can carry my bags the rest of the way," Harriet said.

"I'll be happy to help. This is quite heavy."

"It's full of books," Harriet said. "I'm prone to insomnia, so I don't like to be anywhere without a good book. But it's hard to know what kind of reading mood I'll be in."

"I'm sorry to hear about your insomnia." *And surprised*, Liz thought, since Harriet had been so full of dream stories. "Perhaps you should buy an electronic book reader. Then you could carry a whole library of books without any extra weight."

Harriet wrinkled her nose. "But are they really books?"

"I think it's the stories inside that count."

"Actually, I slept quite well here, except for the disturbing dreams." She reached out and took Liz's arm. "I do want to tell you about my last one."

At least it's the last one. "Of course." Liz put the suitcase on the floor, enjoying the moment of rest. "Please do."

"I dreamed that you were chasing someone," the older woman said. "The person kept pulling off mask after mask, each time making you think it was a different person."

"That's an interesting dream," Liz said.

"After Brya showed us the picture of that masked figure this morning, I knew you needed to hear about my dream."

Liz did find the dream an eerie coincidence. "I appreciate that. I promise to be careful."

"Good." Harriet launched herself toward the door. "I must say I had a delightful time. This inn is much more exciting than the places I've stayed in the past. I'll definitely be back."

Liz struggled along behind her guest, glad that someone enjoyed all the excitement. After she got the heavy suitcase loaded into Harriet's car, Liz dashed into Sew Welcome to ask her friends to keep an eye out for the handyman who was coming to replace the window.

"I don't want to miss him when he arrives," Liz said, "but I need to go up and clean Harriet Vale's room. She just checked out."

Sadie turned from where she was straightening the button rack. "Isn't Sarah here?"

"She and Isaac are working at the Borkholder farm today," Liz answered. "It's all hands on deck for some early picking."

"Farmwork is like that. It comes in bursts of frantic activity to bring a crop in," Sadie said. "Don't worry. We'll watch for the handyman."

"I expect he'll pop in here first anyway to say hello," Mary Ann said.

After thanking them both, Liz stopped at the utility room for cleaning supplies and a change of sheets, then hurried upstairs to clean

Harriet's room. When she reached the upstairs landing, she nearly ran right into Brya who dashed from her room. "Careful," Liz said, nearly dropping the bucket of cleaning supplies.

"I wanted to talk to you," Brya exclaimed, her eyes bright. "I want to help catch the ninja. My night-vision camera can be used as a trail cam too. We can put it out in the bushes."

"A trail cam?" Liz asked.

The little girl bounced on her toes. "It'll take pictures when something passes in front of it. And I can send the pictures right to my mom's laptop, like an alert. So we'll know when the ninja is outside."

Liz thought about the idea for a moment. "I don't think your mom is going to want you involved with trying to catch a prowler."

"She won't mind," Brya declared. "It's educational."

Liz wasn't quite sure how that would be educational, but she promised to think about it. "I have to go clean now, but I'll let you know."

Brya wrinkled her nose. "Cleaning isn't much fun."

"Not so much," Liz said. "But it's important. You wouldn't want to stay in a dirty room."

"That's okay. I have to go finish my dragon scales anyway," Brya said. "I'll be in my room, unless I go down to the sitting room or the library."

Liz watched the little girl skip back to her room and wished she had an injection of the child's energy. She continued on to Harriet's room and the task ahead.

After the room was clean, Liz debated between more upstairs cleaning or waiting downstairs for the handyman. She decided to do the downstairs dusting, then zip through the occupied rooms, changing towels and emptying wastebaskets. "But first," she muttered under her breath, "coffee."

She was in the kitchen pouring a cup when she heard a knock at the side door off the utility room.

Beans hopped to his feet and barked low in his throat, heading toward the sound.

Assuming it was the handyman, Liz tried to head off the dog. "Don't scare the guy," she commanded. "We don't want him to leave."

Beans paid her no attention at all, running into the utility room on his stubby legs far faster than Liz would have expected. She followed him to the door, where Beans barked again, his tail wagging. Liz spotted a familiar figure through the upper window of the door. Chief Houghton.

She gently shoved Beans to one side with her foot, so he wouldn't rush the door when she opened it. "Good morning. I wasn't expecting you."

"I wanted to update you," the chief said. "Before you called my office."

Liz's eyes widened. "I wasn't planning to call your office. I assume you got the photo I sent."

"I did, though it wasn't overly revealing. I have someone poking at it with a computer. Digital-image analysis is outside my technical expertise." The chief glanced over her shoulder. "I don't suppose you have coffee on? And maybe some leftover breakfast pastry?"

"I might have a muffin," Liz said, smiling. "Come on into the kitchen."

She led the police chief into the kitchen and poured him a cup of coffee. "Have you solved the murder?"

"Not exactly." He took a sip of coffee. "But after we were finished out in the parking lot, I went up to talk to the jury clerk. She wasn't there. She left early, though no one seemed to know why. One clerk told me toothache, and another said it was a doctor visit. And none of the clerks seemed able to get into her computer to retrieve the list of jurors from your group, so I will have to wait to check that out until the clerk is back. Honestly, I think that's a long shot."

Liz shrugged. "The clerk probably got scared once it sunk in that she really was in danger. And she was nervous about talking to you. She thought it might make her more of a target. I hope she's all right."

"I'll run out to her house later today," Chief Houghton said.

"She may have gone to stay with friends or family. That's what I suggested."

"Thanks. If I can't find her at home, I'll question her at work on Monday." The chief took another sip of coffee, then glanced around the kitchen. "Didn't I hear talk of a muffin?"

Liz laughed. "Of course." She brought him an apple muffin with a sweet streusel topping.

He looked it over appreciatively, pointing. "I like the kind with the crumbly stuff on top. It's messy but good."

"The two often go together." She watched him take a bite and waited patiently until it looked like he could speak. "I don't suppose you heard about the brick through my window."

The chief held up a hand and chewed faster. "I did. I took the brick out to Mr. Wexler's house. It looks similar to the ones his house is made from, but I've seen that exact same brick on half a dozen old buildings around town. There's some at the police station, some at the courthouse." He frowned. "Maybe the library. I'm not sure."

"I don't think I'm being stalked by the librarian, so it probably doesn't matter," Liz said. "Couldn't you run some kind of tests like they do on television? Chemical composition of the brick and mortar, things like that?"

The chief chuckled. "In Pleasant Creek, Indiana? I'm not sure they even do that kind of thing in the city, not for something like a brick through a window."

"Not even for one that is tied to a murder?" She crossed her arms. "Plus, there may be many buildings with brick in this town, but how many are undergoing renovations? We know Will has access to the old brick coming off his house."

"True, but so does anyone who knows him. They're scattered around the yard," the chief pointed out. "Right now, the brick isn't much evidence of anything, except proof that someone doesn't like you. We can find out how many brick buildings in Pleasant Creek are being renovated. I'll put Officer Gerst on it. He's an eager beaver and a big fan of yours."

The chief finished his muffin, then declined when Liz offered him another.

"I have to watch my weight," he grumbled, patting his ample waistline. "I'm starting to hear rumors of an unflattering nickname going around the station."

"Oh?"

"Forget it. I'm not sharing that intel." The chief drained the last of his coffee and promised to let her know when he found the jury clerk. Then he left.

After Liz cleaned up the kitchen, she flipped through cookbooks, searching for something new to bake for coffee hour, when the handyman finally arrived, full of equipment and apologies. The young man looked vaguely familiar, and Liz realized he had put up shelving in Sew Welcome when Liz bought the inn. "Your name is Calvin, right?"

He pushed a hank of blond hair out of his eyes before sticking out his hand to shake. "Yes, that's me. Sorry I couldn't come before now."

"Mary Ann said you were very busy."

"I never seem to have a steady amount of work," Calvin said as he lugged his tools to the four-season room. "It's either feast or famine."

"Thanks for fitting me in," Liz said. "I enjoy sitting in this room in the evening. It has a beautiful view of the lake."

"It is a right pretty view," he agreed, hardly glancing through the window before turning his attention to the frame. "I should be able to get this set up quickly. It's a good thing Mary Ann measured the window. I was able to get the glass cut and bring it with me."

Liz looked at him in surprise. She hadn't seen Mary Ann measure the window. She thanked the young man and left him to the job, walking back to the quilt shop. "Your handyman friend is here."

Mary Ann handed a bag to a smiling customer. "I'm glad. He's actually the son of a friend of mine from church."

"He said you gave him the measurements for the window," Liz said. "I never saw you measure it."

Mary Ann smiled. "He asked when I talked to him, so I took measurements then. You were doing something else. By the way, I need to warm up a pie before the Material Girls meeting. Will that be all right?"

Liz lightly smacked herself on the forehead. She'd completely forgotten the meeting of the quilting group. With everyone in the group equally pressed for time during the busy summer months, they had to squeeze meetings in whenever they could. "I'm glad you reminded me, or you would have had to come looking for me when it was time."

"You've had too much on your mind. So, using the oven is okay?"

"Of course." Liz grinned. "Anything for pie."

She chatted with Mary Ann a little while longer. Sadie joined them after finishing up with a customer who wanted a specific type of quilt pattern but couldn't provide any details to help find it. "I do love a good puzzle," she said.

"Normally I do too," Liz admitted, "but my life has been too puzzling this week."

Mary Ann's sweet smile faded. "I have to admit, I could do without any more bricks through windows. That was terrifying."

Liz agreed, and they pointedly turned the conversation to cheerier topics until a group of excited customers came in, full of quilting questions.

Liz left Mary Ann and Sadie to their work and headed back to check on the four-season room window. To her surprise, the glass was in place and Calvin was mostly done.

"You work fast," Liz told him. She glanced down at the indoor-outdoor carpeting and noticed a dirty shoe print on the carpet and one right in the middle of the rattan love seat near the broken window. She walked over and began smacking at the dry dirt on the love seat.

Calvin pointed at the dirt she knocked to the floor. "Those aren't my dirty prints. I cleaned my feet on the mat after I stomped around your hedges. The soil is soft and really gets in your shoes, but I was careful. I've been doing this long enough to know better than to track dirt into people's homes."

"I believe you." Liz studied the location of the two shoe prints and remembered Brya's photos of the ninja. Had the person lurking in the bushes entered the inn through the broken window? If someone had, the love seat would be a logical stepping-stone from the window ledge to the floor.

She wondered if she should call the police to take photographs of the remaining shoe print. They could compare it to the shoes of everyone connected to the case. She looked ruefully at the dirt on her hand. At least she still had one print.

The door to the four-season room swung open, and Beans barreled inside.

Liz walked over to close the door, not wanting any of the guests to come in until she got a photo of the shoe print.

"Wow, what a great dog." Calvin leaned down to pet Beans.

The dog flopped over and rolled around directly on top of the shoe print beside the love seat.

By the time Liz could get the tubby dog off the shoe print, it was completely rubbed away.

With a sigh, Liz gave up and patted Beans on the head. It wasn't his fault. She paid the handyman and trudged into the kitchen, only to be cheered by the amazing scent of blueberry pie.

At the Material Girls meeting, the pie turned out to taste every bit as good as it smelled. Naomi had brought some miniature cupcakes to share as well. Between contributions from Mary Ann and Naomi, Material Girls meetings were always as delicious as they were fun.

Liz resolutely pushed all thoughts of the murder out of her head and concentrated on the meeting, right up until everyone pulled out their quilt-block projects. The lap quilt would feature blocks with paw prints in a variety of colors, done in a combination of pieced, appliqué, and embroidery.

Liz took out her own, sheepishly admitting that she had not worked on it at all since the last meeting. Though she'd certainly had a crazy week, she knew that was no excuse. Mary Ann, Sadie, and Naomi ran businesses and had managed to work on theirs. And Caitlyn was a nurse who always seemed to be taking on extra hours, but Liz saw progress on her block as well. She peeked over at Opal Ringenberg, hoping to find the older woman was in the doghouse along with her, but Opal's block looked nearly completed with only some embroidery left.

"I'll put a few hours into my block tonight," Liz promised.

"Do you need any help with it?" Mary Ann asked gently as she threaded a needle with embroidery floss to work on her block. "I could finish it up for you since mine is almost done."

"No, I'll finish it." Liz glanced around, noticing the slightly dubious expressions on the faces of everyone except Mary Ann, whose expression might have been described as sympathetic. "*I will.*"

"The lap quilt is for the Paws and Purrs Charity Arts and Crafts Sale," Sadie reminded her, tucking some raw edge in on her own block and whipstitching it into place. "And it'll be hard for us to donate a quilt with a block missing."

"It won't be missing," Liz insisted as she began neatly stitching a seam between two of the small quilt pieces. "The event is weeks away."

"Weeks that can pass quickly," Sadie persisted.

"If Liz says she'll finish, I'm sure she will," Naomi said loyally, though Liz noticed her expression didn't totally match the certainty of her words.

"I will."

"If Liz needs help," Opal said, "she'll ask for it. She's a grown woman." Then she steered the conversation to the historical society fund-raiser.

"Martha asked me if we wanted to be part of their fund-raiser, though it's really short notice."

"How short?" Caitlyn asked, setting her block on the table. "I'm pretty busy with projects."

"The end of the month. They're trying to raise enough money for renovations on the courthouse," Opal explained. "Martha has a real bee in her bonnet about it. You'd think the building was about to fall down."

"I was at the courthouse at the beginning of the week," Liz said. "It's musty and old, but it seems sound."

Opal glanced up from the row of careful cross-stitches she'd just made. "I believe it is. I think there is some decorative brickwork crumbling. Honestly, I'm not sure where the problem lies. I'm only bringing it up because Martha cornered me and I promised to mention it. I agree with all your reactions. We don't need to be part of this."

"Crumbling brick?" Liz said. "There's a lot of that going around."

"You have brick problems here?" Caitlyn asked.

Liz picked up another piece to begin stitching. "No, someone connected to something I've been dealing with."

"The murder," Sadie put in.

Liz shot her an annoyed look.

"Oh, right. Sadie told us on the phone." Opal leaned forward in her seat. "Any new clues? Do you still think the ex-husband is the killer?"

"We like him for it," Sadie said, showing her fondness for television crime dramas in her wording.

"I don't," Mary Ann said. "All the 'evidence' seems to be fairly circumstantial. The one tangible item you have, the brick, could have come from a number of properties. The courthouse for instance, where this all started." She studied Opal's quilt block. "How are you doing that embroidery? I think I have too many stitches."

The conversation turned once again to the project. Liz tried to focus to catch up with the others, but Mary Ann's words kept coming back to her. She had a point. Liz didn't have any real evidence, but maybe she could get some. All she had to do was provoke the killer into action, which seemed easy enough. Only this time she'd be ready to respond . . . as long as she survived.

21

After the meeting finished, Liz promised again to work on her quilt block as her friends gathered their things to leave. To make good on her promise, she took her project bag into the four-season room and settled into a chair with a glass of iced tea to work and brainstorm her next step. She sat still for nearly an hour until she felt the urge to get moving, and she stuffed the quilt block into her bag and carried it to her room. Her plan wasn't perfect, but it was the only one she could think of.

She fed and walked Beans, rehearsing in her head the conversation she planned to have next.

Beans sniffed a dandelion that had somehow escaped the weeding diligence of her garden helper, Kiera. The pollen from the plant made him sneeze so hard he sat down with a bump.

"I think that's enough outdoors for now," Liz said to him.

Beans clearly disagreed, so she simply picked him up and lugged him into the inn.

Grabbing her car keys, Liz considered asking one of her friends to go along with her. Technically, she was confronting someone who may have tried to run her over and shoot her, so driving over there by herself might fall under the heading of stupid. But dragging Jackson along might keep Will from taking the bait that she intended to lay out because Jackson would be a witness to the conversation.

What she needed was some protection without it being a witness. She stood in the kitchen wrestling with the problem when Beans waddled over and sniffed her pant cuff. Liz thought of the times the little bulldog had rushed to her rescue. "Hey, Beans," she said, making the dog wag his tail furiously, "want to go for a ride?"

She snapped the leash back onto his collar and grabbed the dog carrier that she used when she took Beans to the vet. She wasn't going far, but she wanted him to be safe for the drive.

Beans eyed the carrier in her hand and woofed in distinct disapproval. "It's okay," she said. "No vet this time."

He walked out with her, displaying less enthusiasm than usual, but going along just the same. Once they got to her car, she set the carrier in the backseat and boosted the dog into it. He peered at her mournfully through the carrier door.

"Don't try to make me feel guilty," Liz said. "You won't be in there long."

Beans flopped down with his big head on his paws, his eyes still on her.

Liz was surprised at how busy the streets were on her drive. Of course, it was Saturday in the summer, and Pleasant Creek hosted many different events. As she moved into the pricier residential areas, the traffic thinned some, but one car stayed behind her. Liz glanced at it in the rearview mirror, thinking that if the car's owners lived in the neighborhood, they certainly were frugal since it was a cheap model compared to the sports cars and high-end SUVs that she noticed in almost every driveway.

The car passed her when she slowed to pull up in front of Will's home. His front lawn looked much as it had when Liz was here before, though the pallet of bricks was nearly half gone and several men trooped across the lawn with wheelbarrows. Their sweaty faces shone in the afternoon light, and one man stopped working and wiped his face on the bottom of his T-shirt when he saw Liz park next to the curb.

Liz got out and retrieved Beans as more of the men stopped and watched her quietly. *That's the difference between Pleasant Creek and Boston*, she thought. In Boston, they would have been hooting at her and calling out rude remarks instead of simply watching quietly. Liz led Beans up the walk.

One of the men pointed toward her feet. "Cute dog."

Beans wagged his tail, and Liz said, "Thank you."

The workers turned back to their jobs, and Liz walked on to the front door. Beans followed reluctantly, preferring to stay on the lawn with his admirer.

Will opened the door. "Miss Eckardt." He looked down at Beans. "I'm afraid I can't let you in with the dog. My mother is allergic, and she visits sometimes."

"That's not a problem," Liz said. "I'm fine with staying out here. I came to tell you something."

He raised his eyebrows, giving him an owlish look. "Yes?"

"I think I've found evidence that will prove who killed Nora."

"That's fantastic. I cannot tell you how much I want to see this settled and behind us. Otherwise, it's going to hang over my wedding like a shroud." Will cocked his head. "What kind of evidence?"

"The person broke into my inn and left shoe prints in my four-season room. The police haven't been out to look at them yet." Liz rolled her eyes. "There's some event that is keeping the spare officers busy, but Chief Houghton is sure to send someone out tomorrow. And then all he has to do is check the print against the shoes of every person connected to Nora. The person with the matching shoes is the killer."

Will's bright look faded. "That sounds tenuous. I thought you had something firmer. No wonder the police put it on the back burner."

"It's not tenuous at all," Liz insisted. "And if the police don't take it seriously, I'm sure my good friend Mayor Cross will. We'll match the print to the shoes of the killer." Then she pulled her cell phone out of her pocket and took a picture of Will's feet.

"What are you doing?" he demanded.

"You have small feet for a man," Liz answered. "They appear to be the same size as the tracks I found on my carpet."

Will folded his arms over his chest. "That's enough. I thought you had something real. I'd appreciate it if you'd get off my property and leave me out of your amateur sleuthing activities." With that, he took a step back and shut the door in her face.

Beans looked up at her, his ears drooping, clearly confused by the whole outing.

"It's okay," she told him. "When we get home, I'll give you a biscuit."

At the sound of one of his favorite words, Beans hung his tongue out of his mouth and wagged his tail.

At least someone is having fun, Liz thought as they returned to the car.

Back at the inn, Liz gave Beans a biscuit and left him happily chomping while sprawled on his favorite rug. Making a mental note to vacuum up the dog biscuit crumbs when she came back downstairs, Liz rushed up to the second floor and knocked on the door to Courtney and Brya's room.

No one answered.

The door to the Amish Room opened, and Gwen poked her head out. "Are you looking for Courtney?"

"Actually, I'm looking for Brya."

"They went to an event listed in your brochure," Gwen said. "The cheese-making exhibit at one of the farms." She wrinkled her nose. "It sounded dreadful to me, but Brya is very fond of cheese and loved that particular farm. It's their second trip out there."

"Thanks." Liz couldn't remember when the exhibit was supposed to end. Since it was already afternoon, it was likely they wouldn't be back before dinner. With a sigh, she headed downstairs to begin setting out refreshments for the coffee hour.

To her surprise, her guess was wrong, and the mother and daughter popped into the sitting room by the middle of the coffee hour. Brya skipped to one of the sofas to sit down beside Gwen and started telling her all about cheese making.

Gwen held up her hand. "Sorry, but I have no interest in cheese. I've always thought it was disgusting."

Brya gaped at her. "How could anyone not like cheese?"

"People are different," Courtney said as she took a seat in a nearby chair, "and they like different things."

Brya turned to Gwen. "Do you like ice cream?"

Gwen shook her head.

Brya leaned over to whisper loudly to her mother, "I think she might be an alien."

Everyone in the room laughed, including Gwen, who asked Brya about her wall hanging, launching the little girl into a new, enthusiastic topic.

Liz tried to take part, but it was difficult to focus on the chatter in the room when she was so nervous about her plan. Several times, guests spoke her name sharply to pull her attention to a question or a request.

"Are you feeling all right?" Davidia asked after the second such interlude.

"Yes," Liz said. "I'm sorry for being so distracted. Did you go to the cheese-making exhibit?"

Davidia shook her head. "Though I do like cheese. I took a stroll down to the lake nearby. It was a beautiful day, and I enjoyed hearing the frogs on the lake."

"They really get loud after dark. Sometimes in the spring, I sit in the gazebo and listen to them. It's like they're welcoming the return of warm weather." Liz didn't add that she normally moved her summer night listening to the four-season room where the mosquitoes couldn't reach her. She definitely didn't want to encourage the guests to hang out in that room when she had practically invited a killer to stop by. As soon as she had that thought, she felt her hands go damp from nerves. What was she thinking?

Soon all the snacks were eaten, and the guests started wandering out of the sitting room.

Liz caught Brya before she could leave. "I wondered if I could possibly borrow your night-vision camera."

"What for?"

"I think the ninja might come back," Liz said, "and I'd like to set up the camera where it could maybe take a photo."

"You're going to do my idea," the child said. "A trail cam?"

"Something like that. I want to see the person's face."

Brya's expression grew skeptical. "The ninja wears a mask. Ninjas always wear masks."

"I know," Liz said. "But even if I can only get the person's eyes it might help me identify who it is."

The little girl fidgeted, then glanced at her mom. "I don't know. The car radio said it might rain tonight, and I don't want my camera to get rained on. It's supposed to be weather resistant, but it's almost new . . ."

"I won't be putting it outside," Liz assured her. "It doesn't rain in the four-season room."

"You think the ninja might come inside?" Brya's eyes grew wide. "We should wait for him. I could help."

"No!" Liz and Courtney both yelped together.

Liz tried to soften the harsh response. "I appreciate the offer, but it could be dangerous. And it's going to be boring. I don't even know for sure if the ninja is coming back."

"But you *think* he is," Brya said. "Or you wouldn't want the camera."

"It doesn't matter," Courtney told her daughter. "You're not going to be involved. Now run and get your camera for Miss Eckardt."

Brya looked from her mom to Liz, clearly not happy with either of them, but she finally turned and ran upstairs for the camera.

"You might want to keep an eye on her tonight," Liz said.

Courtney nodded.

Liz spent the rest of the afternoon trying to find things to fill her time. She cleaned up from the coffee hour, walked Beans a couple of times, and even took a walk down to the lake by herself. Finally, the light began to fade, and Liz got ready for what she expected to be a long night. She slipped into the four-season room and sat down in a shadowy corner next to the large potted plant she'd inherited with the inn and had managed not to kill yet.

Time slowed to a crawl, and Liz watched the night leisurely gather against the four-season room's windows.

Hours passed, and Liz was beginning to think she would have to get up and move around a little when she heard a noise outside in the bushes near the windows. The sound could be merely a squirrel or other creature rummaging through the bushes. She knew that sometimes tiny animals could make sounds out of proportion to their size, especially in the quiet night. But then she heard the outside door open. She'd left it unlocked, hoping to stave off any more glass breaking.

Liz held up the camera, intending to take a photo, then call the police, all without alerting the intruder to her presence in the corner. Unfortunately, taking a photo with the unfamiliar camera proved trickier than she expected, and she accidentally activated the small view screen.

Her corner was bathed in the yellow-green glow of the screen.

"Hold it right there."

Liz froze as a flashlight snapped on and shone in her eyes, blinding her. Then she heard the most frightening sound of all, the cocking of a gun.

22

Despite the light shining in her eyes, Liz was able to make out a shadowy figure and a gun gripped in the figure's free hand. The gun pointed directly at Liz.

"I'm sorry," the intruder said.

With that, Liz realized she recognized the feminine voice. It was Sue Thompson, the jury clerk. "Mrs. Thompson?" Liz whispered. "What are you doing?"

She heard a soft sigh. "I have to kill you. I don't have any choice. Not now."

"No," Liz said. "You definitely don't have to kill me. Killing me is only going to dig you deeper into trouble."

"I can't get any deeper. I don't have a choice, but you do. Your death doesn't have to be something painful like a bullet. I don't have anything against you." The flashlight turned away as Sue fished around in her pocket. She removed a bottle and rattled it. "You can take all the pills in this bottle. You'll go to sleep and never wake up. That won't be too bad."

"Fine," Liz said, desperate to keep the woman talking, "but I don't want to die without knowing why."

"Why?" the clerk snapped. "Because you couldn't leave things alone."

"No, I mean, why did you kill Nora? What did she ever do to you?" Then she had a revelation. "Wait, you're Prudence Spratt, aren't you?"

"See? That's what I mean. You can't leave things be. You had to pick, pick, pick." Sue took a deep breath as if to calm herself. "Yes, I'm Prudence Spratt Thompson. Susan was my mother's name, not mine."

"You got married."

"Briefly. That turned out about as well as anything else after Nora ruined my life. She pretended to be my friend. She said we'd take on the world together, but she didn't mean it. She simply didn't want to leave the Amish community by herself. As soon as she'd snapped up her rich husband, she stopped returning my calls. She actually shut the door in my face once."

"So you tried to go home."

"It didn't work. I wanted things the world had. I just didn't want to be all alone." She stretched the last word out into a soft wail.

"That's pretty awful," Liz said. "But murder?"

"I didn't plan to murder anyone," Prudence said. "I was only doing my job, the job I had to take because *I* didn't have a wealthy man desperate to marry me. Being a jury clerk showed me the dark side of humanity so much that I stopped being able to discern the light. I finally married a man I met at work."

"What happened to him?"

"He drank and stole and got himself killed in a car accident. It was exactly what the community said we would find in the world." The gun in her hand trembled. "I got sick after that and spent some time in the hospital. When I got out, the town let me have my job back. I guess I should be grateful. Without it, I probably would have moved away, and then I'd never have found Nora again."

"Did you plan to kill Nora all along?"

Prudence drew herself up sharply, her face a picture of offense. "Of course not. She was my friend. She was practically my *sister*. I was happy." She laughed, a sharp, mirthless sound. "I thought it would be my chance to reconnect with her. Even if she was still married, I figured we'd both changed. She'd appreciate friendship more. I thought it was providence giving me a chance to have my friend again." She paused. "I still think it was providence but with a different message."

"I'm surprised an Amish woman would have a gun."

"I'm not Amish. Not anymore. I haven't been in a long time, and I never will be again."

"But you still believe. You still know the difference between right and wrong."

"You talk to me about right and wrong?" Prudence demanded. "Is it right that Nora ruined my life? In the jury room, she showed no sign of recognizing me at all. We were like sisters, more than sisters, and she barely glanced at me as she sailed into the room. How right is that?"

"Years have passed," Liz said. "People change."

Prudence thrust the gun forward emphatically. "I gave her time to recognize me. I waited, but it was obvious she was never going to even *see* me. She was too busy complaining about her life. She had a wonderful marriage to a good man, but she drove him away and then complained about him."

"You cared for Will Wexler too?" Liz asked.

"No!" Prudence shouted, taking a step toward Liz.

Liz flinched, pushing deeper into the corner and wishing she could somehow get farther away from the clearly disturbed woman.

Prudence took several deep, heaving breaths, then continued as if Liz hadn't interrupted. "I was angry. I was afraid of what I might do, how I might react. I couldn't lose my job. So I left the building. I walked around in the little sitting area outside. I often go there to think when I need to breathe."

"It's a pretty spot," Liz said softly, encouraged by the calmer tone of the woman's voice.

"I sat on one of the benches, and the flowers around it were buzzing with bees. It made me think of Nora when we were children. That's why we were friends. Did you know that?"

Liz shook her head.

"Nora was terrified of bees because of her allergy," Prudence said. "I felt the exact same way about snakes. My brothers teased me about it, an Amish girl afraid of snakes with all the time we spent in the fields. It was silly, but I could not feel otherwise."

Liz thought of Davidia's snake upstairs, wishing desperately she had a way to retrieve it, but squashed into a corner of the four-season room, the knowledge of the jury clerk's snake phobia was as useful as the carpet under Liz's feet.

"We were both afraid of silly things, things no Amish girl would fear. It brought us together, but it wasn't enough. Nora was never really my friend. I know that now. When I was sitting on the bench outside I figured it out. Seeing Nora. Seeing the bees. It was a message. I was supposed to use the bees to give Nora one more chance to do the right thing."

"I don't understand."

"I dumped my medicine into my pocket and caught two bees in the bottle. It was so easy. That's how I knew I was doing the right thing. The bees practically wanted to go into the container."

"Of course," Liz said, amazed at how eager the woman's voice had become. Prudence wanted to believe that she'd seen signs giving her permission for her actions.

"I brought the bees upstairs, not sure when I would get a chance to use them, but then I got the message that the jurors were released. I knew if I was meant to deal with Nora that something would happen. I went to my office and waited, and Nora came."

"She did?" Liz said in surprise. "So she did recognize you."

"She came to my office to ask for a form." The clerk's voice was bitter. "She wanted to be paid for her jury service. She still acted like I was no one. I followed her into the elevator. I wanted to give her one last chance to see me, but she kept punching buttons on her phone and didn't even look at me."

"That must have hurt."

Prudence didn't respond to the comment, apparently too caught up in her own narrative. "I stopped the elevator and asked her why she was ignoring me." She paused, breathing hard as if the telling of her story were an uphill climb.

"What did she say?"

"Why wouldn't I?" Prudence said in a cold and snobby voice.

"Maybe she still didn't recognize you."

"She said my name," Prudence said. "She knew me. Maybe she'd known all along. I'm not sure. I grabbed the bees from my pocket and snapped off the cap, pressing the open bottle to her arm. She tried to pull away, but the bees were so angry. They stung her immediately."

"And she died."

"I didn't know she would die," Prudence said. "She had meds. I let the elevator open on the floor under the jury room. Then I hit all the upper floor buttons and ran up the stairs to get to my office. I wanted to be in my office in case she came out of the elevator and blamed me for what happened. I planned to say she was lying. No one in the jury room liked her, so why wouldn't they believe me?"

"But Nora did blame you," Liz said. "When I thought she was pointing at me. When everyone thought she was pointing at me, she was really pointing at you."

"No one even considered me. After all, you were the one they saw right there, touching her."

"You're the one who killed her."

"I gave her a chance. If Gött forgave her for the horrible things she did, then she would have lived. And if he didn't, then she deserved what she got."

"It doesn't work that way. You know it doesn't," Liz said.

"I know sometimes people have to die who don't deserve it," Prudence said, sounding sad for the first time. "You wouldn't let go. You picked and you poked. You were going to figure it out eventually. I knew that for sure when you came to my office. It would be too hard to make it look accidental. I had to be more direct."

"So you shot at me in the parking lot."

"I was too far away," Prudence said. "But I'm not too far away tonight. You're going to be a hero, you know. You'll die confronting an intruder. People will say you were protecting your home and your guests."

With Prudence working herself up into committing another murder, Liz looked frantically around the room. There had to be something she could use, something she could do. Then she noticed the door to the four-season room. It was open a crack, and she definitely had not left it open. *Who could be there?*

Liz hoped whoever had opened the door had also called the police. She needed to keep stalling Prudence. "You lied to me about the accidents you said you had."

Prudence shook her head. "I really did fall on the stairs, and my lamp cord was frayed. Everything at the courthouse is in such disrepair. It seemed like the perfect way to distract you."

"That was very clever."

"You don't need to flatter me. It won't change anything . . ." Prudence's voice trailed off, and her gaze turned toward the floor.

In an instant, Prudence went from coldly violent to completely hysterical. She screamed and jumped up on the rattan coffee table near the love seat. But she must have timed the jump wrong as she only managed to turn the table over, dumping herself on the floor, where she dropped the handgun.

Liz lunged for the gun, but Prudence had totally lost interest in it and was climbing up on the love seat, still screaming. As Liz rose, the lights in the four-season room flashed on. She spun around.

Brya stood next to the light switch, grinning. "You should always have backup, Miss Eckardt. I learned that from TV."

Courtney and Davidia burst through the door. They'd been awakened by the screaming. Courtney had found Brya missing, and Davidia had found Cleopatra missing.

Brya was cuddling the snake when Davidia walked in. "Don't be mad," the little girl said, handing the snake over to her owner. "Cleopatra was a hero."

"Brya was the real hero," Liz said. "She saved my life."

"When I heard the lady with the gun say she was scared of snakes, I ran to get Cleopatra." She looked apologetically at Davidia. "I know I promised not to take her without asking again, but I didn't really have time."

"I'm just glad she wasn't shot," Davidia said, holding the snake close to her chest.

The rest of the guests showed up as Liz held the gun, not quite pointing it at Prudence. Liz didn't enjoy the feeling of the gun in her hand and was glad the jury clerk showed no sign of any fight left in her. Prudence cowered on the love seat, her eyes trained on the snake in Davidia's arms.

The police arrived soon after while Brya was telling everyone the story of her heroics. Liz was glad to hand off both the gun and the murderer to professionals.

When Chief Houghton heard that Liz had used herself in bait for a trap, his normally affable expression darkened. "You could have been killed."

"I could have been killed in the parking lot too," she said, hearing the weariness in her own voice. "I could have been run over in front of Will's house. Not setting a trap wasn't keeping me safe."

Though Liz knew Chief Houghton would have much more to say to that eventually, he let it go in the face of Liz's clear exhaustion and simply took Prudence away.

One by one the other guests headed back upstairs to bed as the excitement died down.

When Courtney announced that she was putting her daughter to bed, Liz gave the little girl a hug. "Thanks for saving my life."

"Thanks for the best vacation ever," Brya said, making Liz laugh.

By the time Liz returned to her quarters, it was already Sunday morning and she'd never even gotten to bed. She washed her face and changed her clothes, then managed to get breakfast on the table for her guests without burning the inn down. She was pretty proud of that. The discussion at the table focused on Brya's new role as hero of the inn, and Liz felt the little girl deserved to bask in the glory.

Still, when Courtney and Brya checked out, Liz gave a secret sigh of relief. As much as she appreciated the child's rescue, she was looking forward to getting her nice, quiet inn back. She was waving at them from the front window when her phone rang.

It was Jackson. Before Liz could even speak, he said, "I found out the most amazing thing. Actually, my intern discovered it."

"What's that?" Liz asked.

"Nora's friend Prudence Spratt got married. Her name change confused us, and that's why we couldn't locate her for so long. Anyway, we've found her. You won't believe this. Prudence Spratt is the jury clerk."

Liz burst out laughing.

"What's so funny?" Jackson said.

"I have such a story to tell you," Liz said. "How about we meet after church and I tell you all about the one that *didn't* get away?"

OLDE MANSION INN

Special Recipe Section

Turn the page and discover
three delicious recipes featured in this book,
prepared by your favorite
leading ladies in Pleasant Creek!

OLDE MANSION INN

Spice Cookies

1¼ cups all-purpose flour
1 teaspoon baking soda
½ teaspoon salt
1½ teaspoon ginger
⅛ teaspoon cloves
¾ teaspoon cinnamon
½ teaspoon nutmeg
½ cup butter or shortening
½ cup packed brown sugar
¼ cup molasses
1 egg
1 teaspoon vanilla extract
¼ cup granulated sugar

Instructions

Preheat oven to 350 degrees.

1. Stir flour, ginger, baking soda, cinnamon, salt, nutmeg, and cloves together in a bowl.

2. Using an electric mixer, beat the brown sugar and butter on medium-high speed until fluffy. Reduce speed to low and mix in the molasses, vanilla and egg. Add the flour mixture. Mix just until combined (don't overmix).

3. Place the granulated sugar on a plate. Roll heaping tablespoon-sized balls of the dough in the sugar to coat.

4. Place on parchment-lined baking sheet. Use a glass to press the balls to a ⅜-inch thickness and sprinkle with more granulated sugar.

5. Bake for 10 to 12 minutes or until the edges are firm.

SWEET EVERYTHING'S

Signature Chocolate Mint Cupcakes

1½ cups flour
1 teaspoon baking soda
1 teaspoon salt
½ cup cocoa powder
1 cup sugar
1 egg
1 cup water
½ cup vegetable oil
1 teaspoon vanilla extract
2 teaspoons mint extract
1 teaspoon apple cider vinegar

Instructions

Preheat oven to 350 degrees.

1. In a medium bowl, mix flour, baking soda, salt, and cocoa powder well.

2. In a separate bowl, blend sugar, egg, water, oil, vanilla extract, mint extract, and vinegar. Then add to flour mixture and mix until batter is smooth and free of lumps.

3. Bake for 15 to 17 minutes if you are baking standard-size cupcakes. If using miniature cupcake molds, bake for 9 to 11 minutes.

4. Frost with chocolate or white icing.

5. Top with mint candy pieces.

MARY ANN'S
Famous Blueberry Pie

PASTRY INGREDIENTS

2 cups all-purpose flour
1 teaspoon salt
⅔ cup plus 2 tablespoons cold butter or shortening
5 to 7 tablespoons ice cold water

FILLING INGREDIENTS

½ cup all-purpose flour
1 cup sugar
5½ cups wild blueberries
¼ teaspoon almond extract
1 tablespoon lemon juice
1 tablespoon butter (optional)

Instructions

1. In a medium bowl, mix the salt and 2 cups of flour. Cut in shortening until lumps are the size of small peas. Sprinkle with ice-cold water, 1 tablespoon at a time, tossing with fork until all flour is moistened and pastry loosely sticks together (1 to 3 teaspoons of additional water can be added if necessary).

2. Form pastry into a ball. Divide in half and shape into 2 flattened rounds on a floured surface.

3. Wrap in plastic wrap and refrigerate about 40 minutes or until dough is firm and cold, but still pliable.

4. Preheat oven to 425 degrees.

5. Using a lightly floured rolling pin, roll one round into a circle that is 2 inches larger than an upside-down 9-inch pie dish. Carefully transfer rolled-out dough to pie dish, pressing firmly against bottom and side of the dish.

6. In a separate bowl, blend sugar and ½ cup flour. Stir in blueberries and almond extract. Spoon into pastry-lined pie dish. Drizzle with lemon juice. Cut butter into small pieces; sprinkle over blueberries.

7. Roll out the second pastry round and cover pie. Cut slits in it, seal, and flute edges. TIP: Cover edge with a 3-inch strip of foil to prevent crust from burning.

8. Bake 35 to 45 minutes or until crust is golden brown and juice begins to bubble through slits in top crust. Remove foil for last 15 minutes of the baking time.

9. Cool on cooling rack for 3 hours.

Learn more about Annie's fiction books at

AnniesFiction.com

- Access your e-books
- Discover exciting new series
- Read sample chapters
- Watch video book trailers
- Share your feedback

We've designed the Annie's Fiction website especially for you!

Plus, manage your account online!

- Check your account status
- Make payments online
- Update your address

Visit us at AnniesFiction.com